NOV 2018

The Young Desperados

THE YOUNG DESPERADOS

AN IVORY AND ALBERT NOVEL

BILL BROOKS

FIVE STAR

A part of Gale, a Cengage Company

Farmington Hills, Mich • San Francisco • New York • Waterville, Maine
Meriden, Conn • Mason, Ohio • Chicago

LIBRARY OF CONGRESS CATALOGING-IN-PUBLICATION DATA

Names: Brooks, Bill, 1943– author.
Title: The young desperados : an Ivory and Albert novel / by Bill Brooks.
Description: First edition. | Farmington Hills, Mich. : Five Star, A part of Gale, Cengage Learning, [2018]
Identifiers: LCCN 2018014289 (print) | LCCN 2018017745 (ebook) | ISBN 9781432849924 (ebook) | ISBN 9781432849917 (ebook) | ISBN 9781432849900 (hardcover)
Subjects: LCSH: Outlaws—West (U.S.)—History—19th century—Fiction. | GSAFD: Western stories. | Historical fiction
Classification: LCC PS3552.R65863 (ebook) | LCC PS3552.R65863 Y68 2018 (print) | DDC 813/.54—dc23
LC record available at https://lccn.loc.gov/2018014289

First Edition. First Printing: November 2018
Find us on Facebook—https://www.facebook.com/FiveStarCengage
Visit our website—http://www.gale.cengage.com/fivestar/
Contact Five Star Publishing at FiveStar@cengage.com

Printed in Mexico
1 2 3 4 5 6 7 22 21 20 19 18

For my daughter, Tricia, may she fly with the angels

CHAPTER 1

BOOKER CREEK, MONTANA TERRITORY
Well ol' Gus was dead.

"It don't look much like him," Albert said to me out of the side of his mouth as we stood gazing down on the work the undertaker had done. Gus's face was white with powder and his lips as red as a harlot's. At least they wet and slicked his hair back and buttoned his shirt right at the throat, even if it wasn't new. His arms and big hands lay in repose across his chest like he was getting ready to jump into deep water, which, in a way, maybe he was, or had, if death is crossing the River Styx.

"What do you boys think?" the undertaker, a tall cadaverous ghoul of a fellow, said, creeping up behind us, that creaky voice like a door opening on rusty hinges, scaring the bejesus out of us. "Looks like he just laid down to take a nap, don't it? I do very nice work if I must say so myself."

"All he needs now is a wig and a dress and he'd look like a she," Albert groused.

"Say what?"

"He don't mean nothing by it," I said of my friend. "He's just in shock that such a man as Augustus Monroe would have reached the end of the trail so soon. What was it he died of?"

"Death," the ghoul replied, giving us a slantways smirk to show he was quite the wit.

"What Albert is meaning," I explained, "was it his heart gave

7

out, or maybe he fell off a chair while drinking and bumped his head?"

"Or possibly fell out of a harlot's window from the second floor?" Albert said. For we both knew of Gus Monroe's weaknesses for cards, drink, and women.

The undertaker looked as if *he* could lay down in a box and close his eyes and appear deader than Gus, and nobody would know if he was or wasn't.

"No, as often happens to men such as your friend here, he was shot," he said, pointing a long finger to the back of his elongated bony skull.

"Bang!" he exhorted for effect. "Those who live by the sword, die by the sword, only in this case, by the gun, don't you know."

"Who shot him?" Albert barked. "I can't believe anyone would get the drop on Augustus Monroe, gunfighter extraordinaire."

For that was how Albert and me knew him back when we'd first known him.

"A most violent soul goes by the cognomen of One-eye Texas Jack Crowfoot," the keeper of the dead said. "The dirty deed was down inside the Oriental, three doors down and two days back. Word has it that it was a dispute over a woman, or perhaps a gambling debt, might have simply been an insult over the color of a shirt."

The undertaker shrugged.

"Color of a shirt?" Albert groaned.

"Men with guns who drink are given to postures of grandeur and bravado. I suspect that was the case between your friend and One-eye, but who can really say for certain. They said it sounded like a door being slammed shut, and so fast it was over in the blink of an eye."

"I find it hard to believe Gus would allow himself to be shot from behind," Albert protested. "He was a man of great guile and caution."

"Well, that may be," the ghoul said. "But there ain't a horse that can't be rode nor a cowboy that can't be throwed, as they say. I reckon it's the same with gunfighters: there is always someone better, faster, more canny who is expert at blowing out brains. In fact, in my esteem, that seems to be the preferred method of manslayers like One-eye Texas Jack. Least from what I've heard."

He waggled his hoary head even as his eyes seemed to take on a life of their own and bulged from his head.

Albert and I looked at each other.

"Then he was assassinated, is what you mean?" I said.

"Yes, that would be the correct word for it," he said as if someone like me couldn't possibly have a vocabulary containing that word.

"Seems that this One-eye Jack drags around a history of death like it was a string of tin cans tied to the rear of a newlywed's hack, and prides himself in such deadly deception. I've heard that he has so many notches on his gun grips, he has to buy new ones every month or two."

"Sounds like fable to me," I said.

"Well, I hope they hang this bottom-feeder," Albert said. "When will the trial be? Me and Ivory want to be there to watch him hang."

"Jerked to Jesus," I add.

The ghoul blew hard on his beaky nose into a gray kerchief and the noise was like the honking of a sick goose falling hopelessly to earth.

"Trial? Sorry to disappoint you boys, but there will be no trial."

"What do you mean?" Albert said.

"Because the slaying of your friend here was mere prelude to other events that day."

"You best talk straight, mister," Albert demanded, "instead of around in circles. Spit it out." Once Albert got his dander up he didn't hold back his feelings none.

"While Mr. One-eye was dropping your friend here into the eternal darkness, his gang robbed the Citizens Bank and then kidnapped the banker's bride, all in one fell swoop, and made off like, well, like bandits and murderers and kidnappers—cutthroats, blackguards, and brigands."

He cast his forlorn but bulging eyes toward the dusty big plate-glass window of his mortuary that had the words **REKATREDNU YTIC** painted in black letters as read in reverse from the inside. He stared as if something grand might happen, but all that happened that Albert and me could see were two men standing out front talking, a lone horseback rider going one way and a dog the other. The dog had a gopher in its jaws.

"A posse went in pursuit, but they returned two days later looking like they had been whipped by Samson himself," the ghoul said. He raised his bony hands in supplication. "Didn't get so much as a whiff of those desperados, or, if they did, they figured they wanted no part of them. Could be either-or."

"Well dang," Albert said. "What sort of law you got in this town?"

"I really have other business to take care of," the ghoul said. "Why, just an hour ago they brought in Lydia Lovelady, poor thing. She was such a beauty in life, but death tends to rob even the fairest creature of her looks. Got her in there in the back room on ice waiting, and you know, it's not gentlemanly to make a lady wait."

Albert swallowed as if he had a crab apple in his throat.

"What about the sheriff?" Albert asked. "What's he have to say about all this?"

"Oh, he wasn't around when all the trouble went down. Once

word got out that there might be a gang headed this way our dear fighter of crime found reason to engage in his favorite pastime, fishing. Didn't learn a thing about the troubles until he returned the next day. By then, the posse was off in pursuit. I've never known a lawman so adverse to the sight of danger and bloodshed, though he looks promising strolling the streets with his shiny badge and high-crowned hat and scissor-tailed coat. He'll make a fine corpse in that outfit when he passes. I've told him as much."

We turned our attention then back to poor Gus lying there as quiet as silence itself, never again to glance at a handful of cards, or taste a cold beer, or the warm passionate lips of a pretty trollop with a big bottom (the way he told us he preferred them); all the activities he was most fond of. I could but hope he had the opportunity at one or more of those things before One-eye Jack's bullet shut down the show.

"You said this all happened two days ago," Albert said. "How come Gus is not yet buried?"

"Well, he had no money on him, and no kin to pay for the funeral, so I've been keeping him on display and charging a nominal admission—two bits to view the body, or four bits to have your photograph taken with the man." He pointed to a large box camera resting on a wood tripod a few feet away. "Would either of you boys care to get your photograph taken with your friend and have a memento cabinet card?"

"No, damn you!" Albert cursed. "It's obscene what you're doing."

"To say nothing of what this town has done for him," I said.

"Sorry, my young friends, but like everyone else in this old world, I've got to make a living, regardless of the circumstances. Some serve drinks and others shoe horses, or sell the flesh. Me, I care for the dead. After all, somebody must, or else nobody could stand to live here, what with the smell of rotting flesh of the unburied. I'm really doing a service to not only the dead, but the living as well, don't you know. Learned my craft under the preeminent Dr. Holmes during the Civil War. 'Tis why I can display Gus here without fear of smell for days on end." He sniffed the air and looked pleased.

I thought Albert might lose his breakfast.

"How much to bury him?" I said.

The ghoul pursed his lips and rolled his eyes, toting up the amount, then toting it up again over what he might be able to skin Albert and me for.

"Well, I offer two levels of funerals—the simple and the deluxe."

"Explain the difference if you don't mind," Albert said impatiently.

The ghoul showed Albert and me his big yellow mule teeth in something akin to a smile.

"The simple is to dig a hole and put him in a cardboard box and drop him in—fifty dollars, embalming included, of which he has been already. Cash on the barrel head. Ah, but seventy-five dollars will get your friend a nice pine casket and a ride to the cemetery in my new hearse, and if you'd like, I could put in a glass window in the coffin lid for viewing, which would be ten dollars extra. Plus, for another fifteen dollars, the town's official brass band will accompany the procession to the cemetery where a priest will read over the body. I must tell you that the simple service won't even get folks to leave their barstools, but with a band and all, there will be plenty to see Gus off on his journey to the other side. Nothing gets the town in a more celebratory mood than a good wedding or a funeral."

Well, we stood there like two mutes at a spelling contest.

"But, really, what is the price of doing right by an old friend? After all, how many chances will you get to bury your friend, Mister Monroe, here?"

Again, Albert and me looked at each other.

"Let's confer," Albert said and we walked over by the front door.

"What's the total come to for that last burying he said, Ivory?"

"About as close to one hundred dollars as you can make it," I said.

The two finely dressed men with button hats stood outside talking to a kid with a wobbly head, who looked like he was asking them for money, the way they dug around in their pockets, that, or they were gamy and scratching their nether parts.

"Well then, how much we got, Ivory?" Albert asked.

I pulled out our savings, which I kept in a leather purse held by a thong around my neck and hid under my shirt. It was our share of the reward money for capturing the Rufus Buck gang, the ones who'd killed Mr. Sand, Albert's father. We'd run them to ground after much trouble with the help of the now late Gus Monroe, whom we'd hired to back our play, knowing that me and Albert had no experience in the art of gunfighting and facing down desperados.

Gus Monroe was known far and wide for his gun artistry. He even got wrote up in the eastern newspapers as well as the likes of the *Police Gazette* and was said to be the match of such as Wild Bill Hickok and Buffalo Bill. We figured he was our best hope, and, even though he was not there at the death of Rufus Buck, we felt still that we owed him a debt of gratitude for all he'd done, and that such an extraordinary life should not end up as a novelty exhibition for the local rubes. We agreed that we ought to do our best to give Gus a final dignity.

I shook the contents of the money purse into Albert's waiting hands, some script and some coins.

"Count it," Albert said. It wasn't that Albert performed poorly at mathematics, he just liked to fish and hunt more.

I did, and he could see the glum look on my face.

13

"Twenty-three dollars and two bits," I said.

"But we got a hundred of the reward money," he said.

"I know it, but you're forgetting we sent your mother half and bought new hats and these sateen shirts and these gaudy boots with the roses in the shafts. It was an extravagance we could have well done without, but too late now to cry over spilled milk, or fancy shirts and boots."

We both looked down at our getup and were sorry we'd gone overboard. What were boots with stitched roses and sateen shirts and new Stetson hats compared with the burying of an old friend?

"Hindsight is always perfect," Sister Mary Virgin had told me back at the orphanage. She was my favorite teacher there and I often think of her still.

The two men outside made motions to the wobbly-headed boy to skedaddle and then they came inside and past Albert and me and went straight over to the undertaker standing at Gus's remains. In the yawning silence of the large room we overhead what they were saying.

"Such riffraff are at the core of the town's troubles," the one said. "Here is one positive outcome, anyway."

"It's good the country is rid of men of his ilk," the other one said.

"Ilk?" Albert said.

"Means, of Gus's kind," I said. I'd gotten a fair education whilst in the Little Sisters of the Sacred Heart Industrial School for Orphans in Dallas before the old Otero Chavez bought me on account of he needed a helper. Otero carried me back to Last Whisky and taught me the craft of coffin building though he would have nothing to do with the dead who went into them. Last Whisky is where I met and became friends with Albert.

"Yes, yes, it's such a shame that they weren't all shot dead," the undertaker said, "instead of robbing the bank and kidnapping Mrs. Pettymoney."

"Scum!" one said.

"Complete and utter scoundrels," the other said

"I hope some lawmen catch up and hang them all."

"Tsk, tsk," the undertaker concurred.

Albert stared at the pair of swells spitefully as they passed us on their way out. Albert and me approached the undertaker before he could retreat to the back room and the lady-in-waiting.

"Got a question for you, mister," Albert said.

"Do tell."

"Why's a body need a viewing window in his coffin lid?"

We could tell he had no rightful answer, but finally said, "Merely an accoutrement meant more for the benefit of the kin who would want to view him as such."

Albert looked at me and I knew what he was thinking.

"Means like our fancy shirts and boots," I said to Albert, explaining the word. "Something extra, not necessary."

Albert's half-lidded eyes caught the meaning of accoutrement.

"What if you don't put that window in?" he said. "How much does that knock off the price?"

"As I quoted before, it would save ten dollars to not have the window put in."

"Well, I'm sure ol' Gus ain't gonna need a dang window. After all, what's he going to look at down in the earth, worms? Seems to me that's just scandalous."

"We can pay you what we have," I said. "Twenty-three dollars—and two bits."

The ghoul made that honking noise again with his nose like we'd told him an off-color joke.

"Lads, lads," he said. "That wouldn't even cover the cost of the simple plan of fifty dollars. I'm sorry for the loss of your friend, but that's life, I suppose." Then he caught himself and hooted: "I mean, that's death."

I had to stop Albert from striking the ugly fool with his fist and said, "We'll be back with the money. But we want you to stop showing him off like a medicine wagon attraction."

"By closing time, then," he said. "Or else Mr. Monroe will be back on display until I earn enough to plant him, good and proper—no window, no brass band, just a hole and so long Nelly."

I promised we'd be there, with the money, and we got out of that flowery smelling place and out on the street, which was busy with traffic and full of horse apples.

We'd sat down in the shade of the awning of an ice cream parlor next to the funeral parlor (must have been the right street for parlors) like two vagrants, which is pretty much how we felt.

"How are we going to come up with the money, Ivory?" Albert said with a sorry voice.

"I've given that some thought," I said.

He looked up hopeful.

"We ain't," I said. "At least we ain't going to come up with the extra cash for some fancy funeral."

He looked at me with cold distrusting eyes.

"I thought you said—"

"We're going to come back tonight and steal Gus and find a place to bury him ourselves."

Albert's stare turned more quizzical.

"Steal him?"

"You remember when we met?" I said.

He nodded.

"That old Mexican, Otero, what got me out of the orphanage?"

He nodded again.

"Well, he made me a fine carpenter of coffins, and I reckon

16

with some planks, nails, saw, and a hammer I could build Gus a real nice box. Then we'll bury him ourselves."

Albert looked doubtful, his forehead a washboard of wrinkles.

"All well and good, Ivory, but where can we bury him nobody will know?"

"Well, we sure can't bury him around here, or that ol' thief of the dead will probably just dig him up again and put him back on display. It's a quandary we're facing."

"Ivory, I wish you'd quit using all those big words on me, I only made it through the fourth grade before they killed Pa, and even then, I skipped school a lot."

"Quandary means we got a tough decision to make."

"Well, I know that."

"We can leave things as they are and eventually the big ugly will have to bury Gus on 'count of the stink, or *we* can steal the body. But that would probably make us outlaws."

"You mean stealing bodies is a crime?"

"You wouldn't think so, on the face of it," I said. "But laws can be funny, what they allow and what they don't."

"I don't even have to think about it, Ivory. I'm for stealing Gus."

"I feel the same," I said. "First thing we'll need is a conveyance to carry him."

"Wagon," he said proudly. "I ain't totally ignorant, Ivory."

"Nobody said you was, Albert. 'Cept you."

We both grinned then, like raccoons eating watermelon.

"We could trade in our cayuses for a wagon," he said.

"But then what would we pull the wagon with?"

"Got a point," he said.

"Hmmm."

"Could borrow one," I said.

"Who'd lend a couple of scruffians like us a wagon?" Albert said.

"Well, there is borrow and then there is *borrow*," I said.

A fellow right then came galloping down the street holding a severed head out by the hair, yelping and screaming in some foreign lingo like a madman. The really strange thing was, nobody was chasing him like you might have thought.

"You ever see the likes?" Albert said.

I shook my head.

"Wonder if he stole something?"

"The rider or the head?" I said.

He shrugged.

We strolled around town looking for a likely wagon to steal but every time we saw something that might work, we got the willies about stealing it, for there were always watchful eyes.

"We're going to have to wait till it gets dark, Albert," I said.

"Might as well kill time getting something to eat and drink," he said.

We'd given the ice cream shop about two seconds of consideration, then walked up the street to a saloon.

ORIENTAL
ICE BEER 10¢
FREE LUNCH W/PURCHASE

It might seem strange to some, but as long as you weren't wearing diapers or sucking at your mama's teat, nobody cared how old you were long as you could pay and you weren't a woman or a Chinaman.

Me and Albert went in and laid our dimes down on the bar wood and grabbed a plate while the barkeep, a big fat fellow who looked like Santa Clause except he was bald and had no beard, poured us each a glass, then swiped the head of foam off with a paddle.

"Here you lads are, one beer, one turn at the table. Want more, cost you another beer."

We got our food and found a table way off in the corner and sat down and pitched in.

After a few minutes of eating our sandwiches, Albert stopped mid-chew.

"What's wrong?" I said. "You find a cockroach in your sandwich?"

"Didn't that undertaker say Gus was killed in the Oriental? And aren't we right this moment sitting in the Oriental?"

Damn if he wasn't right. But I didn't want to believe it.

"Maybe there's two Orientals," I said. "And maybe this isn't the right one."

"Ivory, sometimes you are too simple in your outlook. You think this dog trot of a town would have two saloons with the same name?"

He had me there.

"I sort of lost my appetite, ain't you?" Albert said, looking a little green around the gills.

"Nope. In fact, I was thinking about buying another beer so I could get another shot at that luncheon meat layout, and these pickles are real good."

"I swear, Ivory, you could eat sitting on a dead mule," he said.

"I could, and I would if that's the only way I could eat, and if I was hungry enough I'd even eat the mule," I said with a grin.

"Look there," he said, pointing at a dark stain on the floor close by the bar.

"You thinkin' what I'm thinkin?" I said.

"I bet that is Gus's lifeblood staining those boards."

"Maybe it's just a lot of spilled beer soaked in," I said.

Albert rolled his eyes at me.

"You see any other such stains anywhere else?" he said.

I didn't.

"Come'n," he said, getting up from the table.

Now, since you might not know much about Albert and me, I should tell you that Albert sported one of his pap's pistols, and I the other, sticking out of the waistband of our trousers, which made us look like young desperados, even though we were hardly that. It's one thing to look a certain way and another to feel that same way. Of course, if we'd had enough hair growing on our upper lips so we could sport them gunfighter moustaches you see on a lot of fellers, well, that might have truly made us look desperate.

"I ain't finished my sandwich yet," I said.

"Take it with you," he said.

Sometimes Albert could be awful bossy, but seeing's how he was so dead set to go, I stuck what was left of my sandwich into my jacket pocket and followed him to the bar.

Santa Claus asked if we wanted another beer when we approached.

"Whose blood stains your floor?" Albert demanded, pointing down at the irregular and large darkness.

Santa leaned over the bar top and peered down.

"Why, that's where the former Augustus Monroe lay giving out his lifeblood after being mortally wounded," he said proudly. "Has brought in a lot of extra business, folks coming in just to see where he had his last beer."

"And how was it this happened?" Albert said.

"Why, One-eye Texas Jack murderized him. Just walked up and popped him in the melon. I damn near jumped out of my boots it was so sudden and startling—like a clap of thunder or an unexpected poke in the ass."

"You seen it, then?"

"Seen it? I had half his brains all over the front of my shirt. Was no time to warn Gus. He dropped like a stone down a well. Dead as you please."

"Why didn't you do something, apprehend the slayer?" I said.

He stared at me as if I was a curiosity.

"Say, you're a colored boy. We don't allow no coloreds in here. Didn't you read the sign out front? Says, 'Women, children, Chinamen not allowed.' "

"I can't read," I lied.

"And that sign don't say nothing about coloreds," Albert protested.

"Well, it damn will soon as I can write it on there," Santa barked. "Go on, get out of here!"

"Well, then give me back my dime," I said.

"Too late," says he. "You done et and done drank your monies' worth, hit the skids, you scamps."

"I can bring it back up and leave it for you if you'd like me to," I said.

His big fat face turned red as a vine-ripe tomato.

"You do and I'll beat you with a broom handle. Now get on out of here!"

He started to come around the bar and I grabbed Albert by the sleeve and dragged him with me. Who knew what he might do with that big Colt's pistol there at the ready in his waistband, or me either. Guns are pure temptation when so ready at hand. I knew he was aggrieved about poor Gus, but no sense in us joining him over at the funeral parlor.

Outside, the wind blew, causing a chill to come down off the mountains and race across the flat prairie, and the sky was the color of old tin.

"Well, now what?" Albert said.

"Let's go see that sheriff."

"You mean at the jailhouse?"

"Where else might you find a sheriff?"

"Well, most of them hang out in saloons and bagnios or dope

dens, but remember what that undertaker said about how this one liked to go fishing?"

We walked up the street reading the signs painted over doors until we saw one that read **JAIL** in bold black and not entirely aligned letters. I followed Albert inside.

A skinny fellow raised his head off the desk he sat behind, a string of drool hanging from his mouth and his hair hanging down in his eyes. He swiped it away and knuckled weep out of his eyes and combed back his hair with his fingers as he looked at us.

"What?" he said.

"We come to see about the killing of Augustus Monroe," Albert said.

He must have misunderstood, for he said: "Too late, he's already killed, and besides, what would make a pair of boyos like you think they could kill such a man, just 'cause you got those irons sticking out of your pants."

"No, we didn't come to kill him," I said. "We came to find out about the killing."

"Well, what about it?"

"Want to know how come you didn't arrest his killer," Albert piped up.

"Wasn't here when it happened. I was fishing. But a posse gave chase and lost the trail. They robbed the bank too, you know."

"You mean the posse robbed the bank too?" Albert said.

"No, you idjit," he growled, "that feller what shot Monroe, and his gang. Made off with the banker's wife, as well. Stealing women and such is one thing, but robbing banks is another. Robbing banks is serious business."

"So we heard," Albert interjected. "I hope them fish you caught were good and fat ones."

"Oh, they surely was," he said, smacking his lips.

"Instead, you could have maybe stuck around town here and put up a fight," Albert said.

The lawman's eyes narrowed with his displeasure over Albert's comments.

"Well, what the hell business is it of you two wet noses where I was or what I was doing? I could have just as easily been having tea with the Widow Johnson," he said, doing his best impression of an offended man.

"Gus was our friend," I said.

He threw that narrow-eyed glare onto me.

"Friend! Ha. The only friends Gus Monroe ever had was harlots and whiskey and gambling dens, and you little cusses don't look like none of them."

"Leave off with that kind of talk!" Albert said.

"Why, you impertinent snips!"

Albert looked at me the way he always did when he didn't know the meaning of a word.

"Means rude," I said.

Albert's ears got red the way they do when he is real mad, and they are fair-sized ears too.

"Be that as it may," Albert countered, "you failed to discharge your duties as an official of the law and protect the citizenry of this dung heap."

"You want One-eye Jack so bad," he said, as he reached into his desk drawer, found a wanted dodger with One-eye Texas Jack Crowfoot's name and picture on it, and slapped it down on the desk in front of us, "go catch him yourself. There is a five-hundred-dollar reward on him. And when you catch him, send me a penny postcard, would you?"

Oh, he was having a good time at our expense.

"You mean this town put up a fat reward for Gus's killer?"

Albert and me exchanged looks.

"Not for Monroe," he said. "But on account him and his

gang robbing the bank and kidnapping Banker Pettymoney's newly minted wife. It's him what put up the reward. Poor sucker. He just had her shipped here from Mississippi; daughter of some Confederate colonel got gangrene from an old war wound and passed on. Her and Banker Pettymoney just an hour married before it happened. The reception was being held right in Pettymoney's front yard of that big house he lives in. Had tables loaded with all manner of food spread out and a five-piece band. Quite the shivaree and I wasn't invited."

"No wonder," Albert said. "How could you have been when you was off fishing."

"That's right, I was," the sheriff said, knowing he'd skirted the truth that the banker probably hadn't invited him because he was of low nature.

"The way I got the story was while One-eye sneaks up on Gus and plugs him, his gang was making off with the cash. Then with his iron still hot, he rode right into the yard full of guests and snatched her up and threw her across his horse and rode off with her. Now, that's not a son of a gun I'd want to fool with."

Albert and me listened with irritated attention. It seemed like a tall tale, maybe one to throw us off the scent. But five hundred dollars was a passel of money.

"Where'd we find this banker?" Albert said.

"Ha, I suppose you whippersnappers aim to chase down them boys and save the day, is that it?"

"I reckon it ain't none of your concern," Albert said.

"Well then have at," he said, the corners of his mouth webbed with spittle. "Bank's just across the street from the funeral parlor where they got your boy cooling his heels and being displayed like a prize hog at the fair." He grinned, showing us a crooked fence of teeth. "It's that *big* stone building with the *big* glass windows with *big* gold lettering says, Bank. You boys can read, can't you?"

More teeth, believing himself to be a real wit.

I quickly snatched up the dodger and once outside put it in the money purse tied around my neck and shoved it down under my shirt again.

"We might need this," I said.

Once outside the jail, Albert said he should have knocked the stupid grin off the sheriff's face by swiping the barrel of his pap's pistol across his teeth, like Marshal Earp was said to do with malcontents and such. Albert and me knew all about the West's famed gun toters from the tales in nickel books. I told Albert I didn't think it would improve the man's looks any if he *had* cracked him in the teeth.

"Maybe not," he said. "But it might have improved my mood."

We crossed over the wide dusty street, being careful not to step in horseshit that littered the road, and made it to the bank.

Once inside, the place smelled of wood must and money. The last of the day's sunlight streamed in through the big window and drew a stripe to the tellers' windows. Behind one was a teller with a squeaky voice and marble eyes that gazed out from under his wired frame specs. As we stepped up he asked if he could help us while nervously eyeing the handles of our pistols. My immediate response was to say, "No, we just come in to look around and see what a bank looked like from the inside," but I held my tongue, which I've learned is probably the best thing to keep me out of unnecessary trouble.

"We're here to discuss business with Banker Pettymoney," Albert said in his most serious voice.

The clerk glanced once more down at our guns and started to panic, those marbles rolling around behind his specs like they weren't attached to anything.

"About the kidnapping of his wife," I jumped in.

"Oh," he said, with a look of relief.

A large man the size of a circus ape wearing a tight, checkered suit came from behind a small wood gate that separated the front from the rear. I'd judged him to be in his early fifties as far as age. He had a slick dome of a head, but for a horseshoe of oddly colored brown hair, and tiny ears, unlike Albert's.

"Did I hear something about my wife, Antietam?" he said.

"Yes, sir," I said. I'd never heard a woman with such a name.

"The sheriff said your wife was kidnapped about the same instant as the bank was robbed. Said it was by the notorious One-eye Texas Jack Crowfoot," Albert said.

He nodded and started to sweat even as the color drained from his face.

"But how does this concern you boys?" he said.

" 'Count of he also killed our friend, Gus Monroe, who is this very instant being displayed for two bits a head over at the funeral home. We aim to fix things and avenge our friend, and, if you're amenable, get your wife back too," I said.

Albert gave me a quick look when I used "amenable" but I could tell he figured out the meaning.

"Well, I don't see how—"

Albert cut him off.

"Mister," he said. "We've run to ground as bad or worse then One-eye Texas Jack and helped put *that* fellow under. So, don't judge us by our youth, ain't that right, Ivory?" he said, turning to me, and I nodded and said that was correct.

"Well, step on back to my desk and we'll discuss it more," he said, and we followed him through the wood gate, which had a large spring that creaked like bedsprings when he opened it, and again when he let it close. He sat behind a large ornate wood desk and Albert and me took up residence on two wood chairs facing him.

"I would do anything to get my Tittey back," he said through those store-bought teeth so white it wasn't even a guess.

"Tittey?" Albert said.

"My pet name for Antietam," he said morosely.

Darn good thing I kept my studies up of Mr. Webster's dictionary or I'd have a harder time explaining all this.

"We aim to collect the reward you're offering for your bride," I said while Albert nodded in agreement, "but, we can't guarantee we can get your money back, sir. Them heathens might have already spent it all. But if your wife is yet . . ." I didn't want to invoke the word "dead," so I scrambled my noggin for one not quite so dreadful. "If she . . ."

"I understand fully," he said, reaching into his bottom desk drawer and producing a bottle of what looked like water but what we would soon learn was gin; he set it atop his desk, then reached back in and took out three shot glasses and set them next to the bottle, neat as you please, and poured each one full to the brim without spilling a single drop.

He urged a glass each to Albert and me and took up the remaining one for himself and drank it back.

"She may well be dead," he said. "Men like that, well, they plunder and ravage and kill, do they not?"

We both nodded and his eyes fell on our glasses, meaning we should go ahead and drink them back, and we did, and I have to say this gin stuff wasn't too bad, either.

His mouth gaped open to drink back the second glass he'd poured for himself, me thinking that when I got old, I would be able to afford a fine set of teeth like his, for age should be no reason to let a body's appearance go to seed.

"Ordinarily," he began, "I'd probably tell you boys to go and find a dog to play with. But truth be told, there's not a man in this town has the walnuts to chase after that terrorist and his gang. They're all a bunch of frightened nincompoops. I've wired the Pinkerton Detective Agency up in Chicago, and they said they're sending a man. But every day that passes and he's not arrived is one more day my sweet Tittey is at the mercy of that brute. And lord only knows what privations he will visit upon her."

The old man looked defeated and poured another shot of gin in his glass and one more each for Albert and me. We followed his suit and knocked them back. After a few minutes, even though that liquor had no real kick to it to start with, it had begun to sneak up on me so that I felt like going out into the street, throwing my hat down, and dancing around it the way Otero had taught me, what he called the Mexican hat dance, right in front of everybody. I don't know why I felt that way, I just did. I also sort of wondered why the banker hadn't gone in pursuit of his wife, but then looking at him, his age and bulk, it all sort of explained itself. A good trotting horse might have bounced those store teeth clean out of his mouth.

"Tell you what, sir," Albert said becoming slightly cross-eyed from the gin. "Me and Ivory here will go get the devil who stole your bride. And just bring her back if she's . . . well, you know. We'd just ask that you do one thing for us and swear it on your honor."

"What's that, son?"

"See that our friend, Gus Monroe, gets the deluxe burial, the kind with the little window in the coffin, the brass band, priest, and a nice headstone. You can deduct it from our reward money."

"But what if you don't catch the scoundrel and bring back my wife? And what if she's ruined for the marital bed? And what if the two of you are slain like your friend, then what?"

Hmmm . . .

"Well, like we said," Albert continued, "we can't do nothing about the ruination of your bride, that'd be between the two of you to work out once we got her back for you. And if me and Ivory here are slain, well, I guess it won't matter about ol' Gus, he'll just somehow have to see his own way clear to the righteous source of his beginnings."

I thought it was a heck of an answer Albert came up with. I always did feel that Albert was better at talking when he didn't think too hard what he was going to say first.

"We'll just need you to let that corpse keeper up at the funeral home know you'll take care of the expenses before it gets too much longer," I interjected. "Ol' Gus is starting to turn darkly around the eyes from all that arsenic was pumped in him. Another few days, he'll be blacker than me."

This he pondered on for a minute or two while having his third swallow of the good stuff and I wondered how a fellow could drink so much and still count the cash drawer at the end of the day.

"Well, might you two have something to put up for collateral?" he said after deep thought.

Albert gave me that look.

"Means worth the amount he'd pay for Gus's funeral in case we end up getting murdered, or otherwise don't make it back."

Albert's ears flushed red. Cherry red.

"Mister, we come here to do you a good turn—something nobody else in this dogtrot is even willing to try, and you want us to put up—"

"Collateral," I reminded.

"Yeah, that?" said Albert. "Well you can just go to Hades and sit here and wait for some detective to come all the way from Chicago, if he comes at all, and in the meantime, every day and night your dear sweet innocent wife is in the clutches of One-eye Texas Jack and at his mercy, the Lord only knows the ways he might ruin her out yon in the far wild." Albert swept his arm out, for dramatic effect, I suppose. "Well no thanks to that. It's me and Ivory will be doing all the risking while you sit here drink that, whatever it is in that bottle, and ruminating about what might have been. See you around, Pettymoney. Let's go, Ivory."

And with that Albert stood and turned for the gate and beyond it, the front door, and beyond that the rest of the West, I reckon. And I stood too, but immediately wobbled back down only to stand again, that front door looking like a mile away.

I further knew the workings of doubtful men such as the banker, men who pitted love against money interests, and most of them chose the money. A fellow with riches can always get himself another woman or anything else. But Pettymoney surprised me.

"Wait!" he said. "Please. I'll do as you ask. And if for some untoward reason you aren't able to pay it back—well, it's worth it to me to take the gamble."

Then he took a metal-framed photograph of his wife, "Tittey" as he called her, short for the battle of Antietam, named by her father for a battle during the big war, a name familiar to me for it was how I became an orphan, at least one story had it. Supposedly my pap went and joined the Union soon after Mr. Lincoln liberated the slaves. I was but one years old when Pap took a Confederate's bullet; that was one of Ma's stories. It might not have been true at all. He could have just as easily been shot in a game of poker or for stealing mules, or simply run off to start a new life somewhere. Whatever the truth was, Ma couldn't take it and drank mercury and hence I ended up at the orphanage.

Albert and me stared down at the face of a pretty woman looking straight back at us as if saying "Come and get me." She had ringlets of light-colored hair and a smile best described in Mr. Webster's dictionary as winsome, a high-collared blouse and a heart-shaped locket resting just at the swell of her bosoms.

I felt nearly obscene staring at her. And I thought I'd have to shove Albert's eyeballs back in his head.

Banker Pettymoney tapped the picture with a horned fingernail and said, "I gave her that gold locket as a wedding present."

We both nodded sympathetically. Albert pocketed the picture and we shook hands with the banker and promised to wire him of our progress on a regular basis and of any news we might have.

Once outside again, I was the first to speak.

"Are you crazy?"

"Maybe," Albert said. "But what choice did we have?"

"We could have stolen Gus's body is what and maybe not go and get ourselves killed, is what."

"And spend our last few dollars on a saw and plank boards and hammer and nails. And, don't forget, we'd not only have to steal Gus, which I'm not sure you and me could carry, big as he is, then steal a wagon to cart him off with, Ivory. Don't forget the dang wagon, which could land us in some stinking hoosegow breaking rocks and eating bread and water until we're as old as Pettymoney in yonder and without the benefit of those pretty teeth, either."

He had a point. Least this way, we were assured that Gus would get the deluxe funeral whether we succeeded or not, and if not, enough time to come up with the money to repay Banker Pettymoney. One way or the other, we'd be sure Gus got the coffin with the window in the lid and a brass band.

"Besides," said Albert, "didn't we take down Rufus Buck and his gang?"

"But we had more than a little help along the way," I reminded.

"So, if we need, we'll get more help this time, too."

Hmmm . . .

"Where to start?" I said.

"At the jail, of course, see what we can pry out of that slobbering sheriff as to One-eye Texas Jack's hidey-holes and habits, etcetera. Surely he must know more than we do about such."

I was highly impressed with Albert's use of the word "etcetera," and how he was taking the lead, so that's where we started: the jail.

CHAPTER 2

Back at the jail again, the sheriff was engaged in a game of checkers with a fella no larger than Albert or me. He was sitting under a crashed-in stovepipe hat.

"Your move," he said to the sheriff, who looked like he was trying to figure out how them Egyptians built the pyramids instead of seeing he had a triple jump right in front of him.

He jerked that skinny head up and glared at us.

"Jesus, Mary, and Joseph!" he brayed. "I thought you boys would be gone by now. Why ain't you? And the better question is, what are you doing back here disturbing my pleasure?"

The other fella looked up too. He was young. I guessed he wasn't but a couple years older than Albert and me. He had a lantern jaw and blue eyes and his front teeth stuck out a bit like a squirrel's, which overall gave him an unusual visage.

"Howdy," he said, friendly-like.

We said howdy back.

Funniest thing was, it was a real hot day and this little fella was wearing a jacket over a vest over a striped sweater. A big white kerchief the size of a tablecloth was draped around his throat, and he had a gold watch chain across his middle, the watch hidden from sight. Further he wore a bullet-filled gun belt and leather holster showing off the butt of a pistol. Oh, and a silver pinkie ring. He looked set for the dance.

"Billy, these are the two yobs I was telling you about," the sheriff said.

"Well, now," this Billy said with gleeful blue eyes.

"Well, now what?" Albert said back.

"Oh, just that Sheriff Chugwater here was telling me that you boys are friends of Gus's. My condolences all around, I just come from over to the funeral home to pay my respect. Why, Gus wasn't a bad sort, what I knew of him, and he passed out of this world I'm betting much surprised, as most do who are snuck up on and shot in the brains. I've seen it myself a time or two. There is something comes over a man's face when he realizes he's been fatally shot or stabbed, even for the briefest instant. It's kindy like somebody telling him his wife was found in bed with another man but he don't have time to do anything about it. It must be a terrible feeling. They say Gus was dead before he hit the barroom floor, but, there was that time until he hit it that he had time to think. Just an instant, but still time, as all men do."

He sure could palaver, this kid with the funny hat.

"Well, how good a friend was you to Gus?" I said.

"Oh, we was more like casual acquaintances. Me and Gus got in and out of trouble a time or two, shared a few laughs and bawds, but we weren't like blood relations or sweethearts. Why do you ask?"

"Just wondering why you didn't avenge his killing, is why?" Albert said.

"Why, I would have had I been here, but I was elsewheres when it happened."

"Seems so was everybody else," Albert said.

The sheriff was still trying to figure out his next move on the checkerboard.

"I don't recall him ever mentioning anybody named Billy, do you, Albert?"

"Well ol' Gus had lots of friends," Albert said. "And just about as many enemies too. Lots of gun artists wanted to rub him out just for the reputation of doing so. It was Gus's poor luck the one who did it didn't face him head on. Hell, I even warned him to watch his back at all times. I guess he forgot."

"Gus was getting long in the tooth," Billy said. "Old folks ain't always so cautious as they should be. Take a fella of a lightly step, he will some day trip and break his ankle, and old women forget to wash and old men too. Their mental faculties get old right along with 'em. It's a sad state of affairs but true. I hope I never get old."

Something about this little fella left me feeling skittish as hell. He was baby-faced, kinda like Albert was, but there was something fatal lingering behind those blue eyes.

"Chug tells me you two boys might be going after One-eye Texas Jack for the reward money?"

I knew what Albert was thinking when this Billy brought up the subject. He's thinking that the skinny sheriff ought to have kept his mouth shut. I was thinking it too.

"We're thinking on it," I said quickly.

"Thinking on it?" Billy said. "Well, thinking on it won't get the job done. Fact is, soon as Chug here mentioned it, I thought I might go after One-eye myself. I'm pretty certain I can best him in a gun duel. But here's the thing: He runs with a gang of cutthroats—maybe six or seven of them at any given time, of which I know personally a few, like Dirty Dave and Bones Waller and a geek named Ten Dimes, any of which won't hesitate to blow you out of them pretty boots. They are a bold and incautious lot and probably the reason they robbed the bank and stole the banker's wife as brazenly as they did. You have to give them their due."

Both Albert and me glanced down. Like most, we keep our pant legs tucked into the shafts of our boots to keep them from getting muddy and not have to wash them so often. But, just as much, we do so to show off the roses stitched into them, which

I have come to conclude was maybe a mistake on our part—especially now that this Billy made note of it.

"Hell, where'd you get them, anyway? I wouldn't mind having a pair myself."

Albert started to answer but I interrupted.

"Got 'em in Tascosa," I said. "Last two pairs like these they had. We was lucky, Albert and me, they were just the right size too."

I told him this because I didn't want him to copy us, but I didn't know why I didn't. I thought they looked foolish now, made us look like pimps. This Billy wasn't the first one to make mirth about our fancy boots. We came near to getting into more fights over those boots and our shirts than if we'd gone around slapping the wives of Christians in church.

"Tascosa!" he barked. "Why I've been all over that country—practically my second home. Ain't that something, Chug?"

The sheriff looked disgruntled.

"We playing checkers, Kid, or having a hen party?"

"Oh, Chug, don't be like that now," Billy said. "It's just a checker game. Why it's been some time since I've met anybody who's been to Tascosa. Say, do you two boys know Charlie Bowdre?"

We shook our heads.

"How about a tall drink of water name of Tom O'Folliard—Irish cuss got a funny accent and goofy grin?"

We shook our heads.

"Well drat. Them's two of my best friends. Use to the three of us run over to Tascosa and do some cattle and horse trading. Lively little place. How about did you ever drink in Lolita's Cantina? You'd know it if you did, she's got them out to here." He demonstrated by holding his curled fingers way out in front of his chest.

We nodded, remembering that particular woman.

"One time, yes, to celebrate when we bought our boots and hats."

"And you're right about the top of her," Albert added. "Biggest bosoms I ever saw on a woman."

"Well, dang," said this Billy. "That's where we always drink whenever we're in town. How about did you ever take a turn with Lolita herself?"

We shook our heads.

"Oh, boy," he said, rolling his eyes. "You ain't really lived until you spent a moonlit night with Lolita. You'll feel rode hard and put up wet."

Sheriff Chugwater was starting to look like a bulldog with a toothache.

But Billy had this look in his eyes, dreamy like, as he spoke of Lolita. What I remembered of her was that, in spite of her extraordinary chest, she was as ugly as a mud toad.

"No," Albert said. "We didn't stay long enough for the pleasure."

Albert was learning to lie almost as good as me. I mean, no, we had nothing to do with that wart-faced woman, but we let Billy think maybe we had been around the block a time or two, and thus creating the picture of us as young desperados.

"Well, you know something," Billy said. "I think we ought to throw in together and go and fry One-eye Texas Jack's bacon and get that poor woman returned. I mean, fill him so full of lead he'll leak like a sieve. What'll you boys say?"

"We'd have to talk it over, Albert and me," I said.

"Well, before you do, let's saunter out back into the alley so I can show you something."

I was starting to get a dark feeling, but Albert was eager to go. And when we started out the back door of the jail, I saw Sheriff Chugwater sliding around the checkers so he could cheat—so dumb he screwed up his three-checker jump.

Once outside, Billy pointed down the alley about forty paces and said, "You see that big rat atop that trash?"

We nodded.

And, before we stopped nodding, Billy had relieved the holster of his gun and slammed a shot into the rat, tearing it up so bad its mama wouldn't recognize it. And then a bunch of other rats started scattering—cousins, maybe—and Billy sent four more to rat heaven, *bang, bang, bang, bang,* just like that— fast as lightning and my ears started ringing like I was standing in a church belfry on Sunday morning.

Billy ejected the shells nearly as quick and holstered his six-shooter with smoke still curling out of its barrel. Albert and me both took notice of the odd-shaped handle.

"What sort of dang kind of gun is that?" Albert said real loud because, like me, he was still having trouble hearing.

"It's a bird's head Colt Thunderer," he said. "Real sweet gun and it fits my smaller hands." He displayed his hands; they were way smaller than my own. I always did have big hands and big feet from the day I was born. I got teased a lot on account of it too. Albert's hands were what I'd call normal size for a boy his age, which was around sixteen, or maybe seventeen; birthdays was something I wasn't keen on, not even my own, and I never thought to ask Albert his.

"Them's some good-looking guns you boys are carrying, also, looks like a matched set," Billy complimented. Albert told him they used to belong to his pa, who was a lawman, gunned down by Rufus Buck and his gang.

"Yeah, I heard of them fellers," Billy said, real serious. "I heard Buck used to get dogs drunk, then challenge them to gunfights too." Then he howled with laughter.

"Lord almighty," he said with tears in his eyes. "Sometimes I crack myself up."

Me and Albert couldn't help but laugh right along with him.

He sure had a winning style.

"Well, have you thought over my offer of us throwing in together for that reward on One-eye Texas Jack? Or should I just go it alone?" he said soon as he stopped laughing and fisting the tears from his eyes. "You seen what I can do with a six-gun."

"If you wouldn't mind us talking it over between ourselves," I said, "we can give you an answer in a minute or two."

"Sure, whatever," he said. "I'll just be inside finishing my checker game with Chugwater, that dang fool. He had a triple jump and didn't even see it."

He started in.

"Billy?" I said.

He turned.

"What is it?"

"I think maybe Chugwater messed with the board when we came out here."

He grinned.

"I wouldn't put it past him. He can't play worth squat. Let me know your answer soon, I'm about to fork my pony and ride with the wind. Hell, I never could stay in one place too long."

He went inside.

"What do you think, Albert?" I said.

"We'd have to split the reward," he reminded me.

"Split three ways," I said.

'How much does that come to, Ivory?"

"One hundred and sixty-six dollars and sixty-six cents and maybe a penny or two left over," I said.

"Boy, I don't know how you do that. I thought I was smart, but you amaze me, Ivory."

"I always was good with numbers."

"Well, take him or not?"

"If we don't, he might just beat us there and get all the money."

"Or, he might just get rubbed out, one man against half a dozen, even if he can shoot rats quick as anything. The rats weren't shooting back."

"That's true."

"And then there is that Pinkerton detective Mr. Pettymoney sent for."

"Let's not worry about him," I said. "If we get going right away, we'll be well ahead of any Pinkerton they might send."

"I've heard those Pinkertons are pretty smart fellows," Albert said.

"Then I say, let's take Billy, least we know he can shoot like the dickens and has a good sense of humor."

So, we left out that very day after getting Pettymoney to front us an advance so we could buy a mule to pack supplies with. Billy allowed that it was lonesome country we were headed into and he didn't like going hungry. And to tell the truth, neither did I.

Billy also said that he sort of knew of One-eye Texas Jack's hideout. Called it the "Robbers Roost." Said it was either somewhere in the Dakotas or possibly in Wyoming, he wasn't exactly sure which.

"Sometimes it's dang hard to tell where one place ends and another starts on account all that country pretty much looks the same. Generally, I have to ask somebody where I am if I don't know, and you'd be surprised at how many of them who live there don't know, either. Now I pretty much know New Mexico and where it ends and Texas begins, on account of me and my pals trading cattle and horses back and forth," he said with a wink. "But the rest of this land, well, hell, grass is grass and mountains and rivers and such are just mountains and rivers."

Albert and me looked at each other because on this last, Billy didn't sound positively too certain where this Robbers Roost was.

"Heard of it," Albert replied.

"You mean you heard of the Robbers Roost?" Billy said.

"No, Dakotas and Wyoming," Albert said.

Billy laughed so hard he near fell off his horse, and I near fell off mine too, though I don't know why I found it funny, except that Billy had. Then pretty soon Albert was laughing along with us even though I *knew* he didn't know what was so funny. I'm surprised our horses and the dang pack mule didn't start laughing.

We rode on.

That evening while sitting around the campfire by a little roaring creek, we proper introduced ourselves.

Billy said his first and last true name was William Bonney, but that folks around Fort Sumner down in New Mexico had starting to just call him Kid, though he didn't care for it much. Albert told Billy his was Albert Sand and I said mine was Ivory Cade.

"Well, those are some fine handles," Billy said. "But you don't mind my asking, how was it you two threw in together in the first place? You sure don't strike me as being brothers."

So, we told him all about being friends back in Last Whisky and about Albert's pa and so on and so forth. Billy fell asleep to our jabbering like magpies. He snored loud enough to wake a graveyard full of dead.

"He's an interesting fellow don't you think, Ivory?" Albert opined.

I nodded.

Then I whispered to Albert, "We best be watchful of him."

"Oh?"

I just nodded.

"Got nothing to go by, it's just a feeling I have about him.

41

You know how I sometimes get feelings about certain folks."

Albert nodded.

"Is it on account of him shooting them rats as fast and accurate as he did?"

"No."

"Being friends with Chugwater?"

"Not that, either. Just something cold behind those eyes," I said real low. "Like as he could turn that sense of humor of his into a rage at a moment's notice—or no notice whatsoever."

"Hmm," Albert mused. "Well, Ivory, you know I trust your judgment on all things fatal and otherwise. I remember you telling me way back when we first met about your *premitions*. So I'll keep an eye on him too."

He meant premonitions, of course, but he said it close enough I didn't bother to correct him. Ever since studying Mr. Webster's dictionary to learn new words, I've become something of an old maid stickler. But Albert is my best friend, so I let it pass.

Then we rolled up into our blankets to seek out sleep with saddles for pillows and the ground for a bed. But it took me a good long while to fall into the darkness of the *netherworld*, as Sister Mary Virgin back at the orphanage called it. Her and me would sometimes sit in the garden while she read passages of some book or other, having said once while on the subject that sleeping was like dying a thousand deaths.

Anyway, this one book she had (and don't ask me why I thought of it just then) was written by an Italian fellow name of Dante. I couldn't possibly understand it all—but it was about death and hell, mostly. Hell and sin, and the netherworld and how you ended up there and so forth.

She said this Dante fellow lived a few hundred years ago, but that Italians were by their nature romantic and moody, especially the men, and they spent a lot of time writing poetry and painting and falling in and out of love, and I reckon trying to fall asleep. And sometimes when she'd talk about these things she'd get a faraway look in her eyes and sigh heavily.

To prove her point, I suppose, most folks who would write about hell wouldn't produce something you'd think had anything good in it. But as Sister pointed out, this Dante fellow was talking about sin and what happens if you don't live a righteous life and fall into sin.

"You must do your best to live a life of goodness and godliness, Ivory, so that you do not spend eternity suffering in hell for a few moments pleasure here on earth. Do you understand about sin and such?"

"Yes'm, I think so," I recall telling her. Of course, it weren't much use her talking to me about the subject since I had not yet had a chance to commit much sinning, unless lies was counted.

One time as we were walking around the big lake there on the grounds, I asked Sister if she ever wished she'd lived a different life, for I'd gotten to thinking about such things in talking to her. I think maybe I was even falling in love with her because she was pretty and kind and gentle and wise. I got to wondering what it would be like if we was to run off together and rent a little house out in the woods and have some chickens and cows. I mean there was a lot of time for a fellow to do some thinking there at the orphanage if he wanted to.

"Children," she mused aloud. "I sometimes wish I might have had children, my own. But it was not God's will. So, you all here at the orphanage are my children and I am not missing out on anything, really."

"Can I ask you something else, Sister?"

"Why certainly, Ivory."

"How do you know what God's will is?"

She blinked several times and I thought maybe it was the sun glinting through the trees into her eyes.

After a moment of silence, she said, "I just know and trust Him, Ivory. We all know what He wants of us if we just pray and listen."

I remember shaking my head and saying, "Not me, Sister. I don't have a dang clue what he wants of me. Fact is, it's hard for me to believe in something I can't even see. I mean, I've heard them stories in the good book all about Jonah being swallowed by a whale and Daniel walking into a lion's den and Samson slaying all them Philistines with an ass's jawbone. Boy, howdy, that was something and mighty exciting. But I don't know how such things could really be, I honestly don't."

She smiled as she always did, ever so sweetly at me as if I was the daftest child ever to come out of his mama—and maybe I was. But I just couldn't know what it was God wanted of me, I told her.

"Of course, you do, Ivory. You just haven't asked the right question of Him yet. You must pray constantly and listen with all your heart for the answer to your prayers, and the answer will come to you eventually."

I had no heart to tell her that the only thing I prayed for was to get out of the orphanage and become a cowboy like what was in the dime novels I read, and thus far my prayers hadn't been answered, not even one. But, then later, they sort of were when the old Mexican carpenter, Otero, come and bought me and taught me to build coffins while he drank and told lewd stories of when he was a young bandit and all the women he had conquested, as he put it.

Often Sister would speak of things with this wondrous far-off look in her eyes. I don't think she even knew she was doing it. But I have always been a close observer of other humans and once almost drove myself crazy by staring into my own eyes in a mirror trying to figure out who I was. I recall asking myself,

"Who's in there?" No answer.

The last time I saw Sister, she was strolling along with her rosary threaded between her fingers and her lips silently moving and no doubt praying hard for something as she headed off to morning Mass. The next day, I heard she had left the orphanage that very night. And later a rumor swirled that she'd gotten with child and went off with a man in a dark suit of clothes and black moustaches driving a one-horse hack.

So, maybe she had finally asked herself the right question and got an answer she wasn't expecting and the Lord sent along this man in a black suit to carry her off to wherever the Lord and this man wanted her to go, then later he sent me the Mexican carpenter, and, like always, I got the short shrift.

I lay there wondering that night with light and shadows doing the two-step of a dying fire, and coyotes serenading way off in the hills, what the Lord was wanting me to ask Him, and thought, heck, I didn't figure it was for me and Albert's fate to chase outlaws the rest of our days and maybe end up shot dead and brainless like ol' Gus. At least I hoped not. And before I knew it, Morpheus snatched me and carried me off.

CHAPTER 3

Bright and early the next morning, I was awakened by Billy singing a fairly good version of "Silver Threads Among the Gold."

A sweetly mournful tune if ever there was any.

"Darling I am growing old,
Silver threads among the gold,
Shine upon my brow today
Life is fast fading away . . ."

And when I sat up out of my blankets, there he was squatted, buck naked in the roaring stream splashing himself with water and rubbing himself with a bar of yellow soap, as if he was in some highbrow hotel bath, ignorant of the coldness of the water. His spotted pony stood close by watching as if it was learning what to do if ever it got a chance to take a bath. It looked like one real savvy horse to me.

Albert's and my ponies and the pack mule cropped grass contentedly near by and I thought how happy horses must be to be ignorant of man's folly and woes—just eat and sleep and once in a while carry somebody from here to there and not worry about a single thing. Cows, the same way, only dumber. Dogs, I figured, were a little different in that when you spoke to them, they'd look you right in the eye and as often as not do what you told them. Now, whether or not they liked it is another conversation. I don't know why my mind goes off on such trails as it does, it just does.

Besides Billy's naked haunches directly in my eyesight, I smelled coffee and saw that Albert had set a blackened tin coffeepot on a fresh fire and had bacon sizzling in the fry pan, watching it as he sat cross-legged Indian style with a green stick in hand to turn the bacon. I admired him a great deal. He was the best friend I ever made.

Early risers. I never could understand why a fella would want to be up so early when they could just sleep in. But now that I saw both of them was up I got up too and shook a scorpion out of one of my pretty boots, then whacked it with the heel, but to no effect; it just scrambled off into the brush. Good riddance.

I eased over to the fire and squatted down next to Albert and poured myself some of that Arbuckle that smelled so good; and damn it was hot enough to scald the skin off a catfish.

Albert motioned with a jerk of his head to where Billy was splashing about and singing that mournful tune.

"Yes my darling you will be,
Always young and fair to me . . ."

"He sure seems to enjoy life, don't he?" Albert said in a low voice.

"True," I replied. "He has a sunny outlook, but then so do fellers who don't see much of a future and just live in the moment."

"Well, maybe that's a good lesson for us all," Albert said.

Billy finished his song, then stood straight up in the creek, the water sluicing off his fish-white limbs, but for the back of his neck and his wrists and hands, which were burned brown as leather from the sun.

I saw that his clothes were drying on a bush.

"Clean as a cat too, ain't he?" Albert said.

"An admirable trait," I said.

I am not much for early morning conversations for I believe that when we sleep, all our parts fall asleep too, and my brain is the last to sleep and therefore takes longest to wake up. So my brain is naturally unable to string too many words or thoughts together at one time early morning. I sipped a couple of sips of the coffee trying not to burn my mouth, then excused myself to go off into the bushes for my morning constitution, also a time for reflection, or reading a dime novel, of which I had none with me but wished I had.

By the time I got back to the fire, the bacon was done and Albert and Billy were using the green stick to pluck strips out and on to some soda crackers. By now my brain had awakened and advised me that I was also hungry so I joined in the breakfast, skinny as it was.

"How far yet do you reckon it is to this Robbers Roost, Billy?" I asked as we were polishing off the bacon and soda cracker sandwiches.

He chewed and thought and chewed some more and took a sip of coffee and swallowed finally.

"Well, I ain't exactly sure," he said. "Figured we'll get on to Deadwood, then ride west from there, or Cheyenne, maybe, where I know a couple of yobs will know how to locate the Roost."

"Yobs?" Albert said.

"Oh, it's what Chugwater calls just about everybody he dislikes, says yob is simply boy spelled backwards. Ain't that something?"

"Well, who are these yobs?" I asked getting into the swing of things, for I am a lover and purveyor of odd words and, sometimes, odd people.

"The Pallor brothers," Billy said. "I never did make their acquaintance, but I hear they are hell on wheels at killing folks, and you know what they say, 'Birds of a feather' and all that."

"How's this supposed to work?" Albert asked. "I mean as it stands, we're already looking at splitting that reward money three ways, five ways makes it even less appetizing."

"Got that figured," Billy said, licking bacon grease from his fingertips. "We won't take them on, we'll just buy 'em a bottle, get them drunk and pry it out of them where this Robbers Roost is. Takes one to know one, I always say."

"Well how far to Deadwood from here, Billy?" Albert asked.

Billy took to chewing on the last strip of bacon, careful not to burn his mouth from the fat grease, and swallowed.

"Maybe two, three weeks' ride if we don't run into Injins," he said.

"Indians?" I said.

"What kind of Indians?" Albert asked.

"Why, there is all kinds," Billy said. "You got your White Mountain Apaches, and your regular Apaches. You got Kiowa and Comanche and Blackfeet and Cheyennes and a host of others. They's so many they's like fleas on a dog. But I'll say this for them, they can all be dangerous, especially to white fellers like us," and he looked over at me, then added: "I reckon they'd be pretty hard on you too, Ivory, seeing's you're with a couple of white fellers like Albert and me."

It was one of those truths that felt sort of like being poked with a stick, though I understood what he meant. On the other hand, it was no relief to know that my particular skin color might not make a difference when it came to being killed.

"After they shoot arrows in you," Billy continued, "they take your scalp. Now yours might be a real trophy, Ivory, all that wooly hair."

"Well, I reckon if you're dead," Albert said, "it don't matter what they do, does it?"

"I thought the army whipped them all?" I said.

"They whipped a lot of 'em," Billy said, slurping and blowing from his coffee cup, as his bucked teeth clicked against the metal rim of his tin cup each time he went to take a drink. "But they ain't whipped them all, not hardly. Why it'd be somewhat like if you and me and Albert here was to try and stamp out grasshoppers in a wheat field with a stick."

"Well, which ones have they whipped?" Albert said.

"The good ones mostly, what will stay on the reservation—mostly them. The worst ones, though, is all the rest. Me, personal, I'd say the Apache, for thems is the ones I know of best. The White Mountain Apaches down around where I hail from. You rile them up, they'll stake you out and cut off your eyelids so you can't close your eyes in order to keep from going blind. Then they'll pour honey on you so the ants drive you crazy. Then, if they ain't tired of funning with you, they'll cut off your tallywacker and make you eat it whilst they roast you over a fire like you was a hog they caught."

Just Billy talking about it caused my nether parts to shrivel up and send shivers crawling down my spine.

"Happened to a friend of mine once," Billy said. "Got up with a 'Pache squaw. Either didn't know or care she was married. Ol' Delray sure found out the hard way that she was, though. Word has it, her buck killed him while he was still topping her—came and went all at the same time, I reckon you could say!"

He rocked back with laughter at the joke, sloshing coffee out of his cup.

Albert crossed himself like the Catholics do, then tossed the dregs of his cup into the fire, causing it to hiss as he stalked off, the color drained from his face.

"Well, pilgrims," Billy said. "We're burning daylight. Best get going. I sure hate to think what One-eye Texas Jack is doing to that banker's bride 'bout now. And I'll lay wager it ain't no good whatever it is—maybe for him, but not for her leastways."

"So, how well do you know One-eye?" I said.

Billy donned his stovepipe hat, and hefted his gun belt over his narrow hips, then buttoned his sweater beneath his coat.

"Poquito," he said holding his thumb and forefinger apart. "That's Mexican for 'somewhat,' case you boys are ignorant of the native tongue. He's a real bad hombre. And many of his gang are just as bad as him. 'Bout the only thing he likes better'n killing, is ravaging. And the way Chugwater tells it, when the banker's bride arrived in town and stepped off the train, she was so comely a wagon ran over half the tongues of the local men. So, if we get her back, she'll probably be well broke in for the bridal chamber, I'm bettin'. But if she's a good enough fibber, Pettymoney might never know the truth. I don't think I would."

"Maybe he will hold her for ransom," I said, trying to remain hopeful for the woman's sake.

Billy snorted.

"More likely take his pleasure, then sell her to Comancheros. Get some decent money for her when he tires of her company. That's what I'd do after I got to know her a little better, so I could vouch for her qualities, if you know what I mean?" He gave us a wink and a grin as he saddled his mount.

"You ever do something like that, Billy?" I said.

He eyed me coldly from across the back of his horse after he dropped his saddle on.

"I wouldn't have to," he said, his voice suddenly serious. "I got plenty of girlfriends who don't mind sharing my bed, and besides, money don't mean that much to me."

"But then why are you wanting the reward?" Albert said.

"Why, Albert, I didn't say I didn't *like* money, I just said it don't mean that much to me. And 'sides, I kill One-eye Texas Jack, it'll be another notch on my gun and one less dirty woman-stealing scoundrel this old world will have to deal with. 'Sides, I'm always up for a good adventure with companionable fellers like yourselves. It ain't so much where we end up—we all know where that is, the grave. For me personal, it is how I get there that counts with me. A body can spend his days rocking in a chair and die of old age, or he can fork his cayuse and go lookin' for adventure and die young."

I didn't much care for the way Billy talked about Mrs. Pettymoney's predicament, so cavalier and all. I felt plumb sorry for the lady and I didn't even know her. I reckon it was the good sisters at the orphanage who taught me about decency and the respect of womanhood. They were some of the best people I ever knew, except for one: Sister Ophelia, who seemed to take great delight in rapping my knuckles or slapping me in the back of the head when I didn't get something correct or she caught me talking in class. A big woman with a moustache some gunfighters would have envied.

We soon had our mounts saddled and the pack mule packed and we rode onward toward Dakota, which was where the mining town of Deadwood was supposed to lay, a place I'd heard much wild talk of, and also had read about in my dime novels. It lay in what was called the Black Hills where General Custer discovered gold that set the Indians off because they considered the hills to be a sacred place. Once word got out about the gold, there was no stopping the miners and others from coming. I felt sorry for the Indians while at the same time idolizing Custer and felt real bad when I read he got his comeuppance not long afterward.

Most evenings we would try and find a fine nice little place to camp, usually in an open glade with plenty of rich grass for the horses and a good stream for water and in no time, we'd fix our fire for coffee and victuals and palaver. I kept hidden my two cans of peaches for the most desperate of times, more to raise our spirits than anything, a time when we all could use something sweet and delicious to cheer us up.

Billy was always regaling us with tales of derring-do as we

rode along and later as we camped. Albert and me, every few days, would wash out our clothes and rinse and hang them over a tree limb to dry. Billy would as often as not just wash his clothes with him in them, then strip down and go about naked while they dried. He said it was a matter of being efficient. He seemed to possess no modesty about being naked. Not like Albert and myself.

"Them's pretty shirts," Billy remarked about our sateen ones we bought along with the boots and hats with some of the reward money we got from hunting down Rufus Buck and his gang. They weren't everyday shirts, though, and the first time Billy saw them he made that comment about how pretty they were.

"Along with them fancy boots," he further said. "Why the wrong crowd would be calling you fannies or weak sisters. Lots of these old cusses out here don't cotton to fancy at all. See it as a sign of a man being weak or womanly, to wear anything but wool and denim and run down at the heel boots."

Albert and me looked at each other.

"I like to gussy up myself now and then," Billy said. "And any man who would make fun of how I look might eat a lead sandwich. You got to be tough out here in this country. Stand up for yourselves. For I will tell you one more secret about some of these old-timers when it comes down to it—they see you as fannies, they're just as likely as try and get you to share their blankets at night."

He winked at that.

"Might come a time you boys have to have more'n a little grit to wear such fancy shirts and boots—unless of course you don't mind sharing a blanket with some crusty old codger."

He built himself a cigarette and lighted it by leaning his face to the fire, then straightened and blew twin streams of smoke through his nose.

"Fact, the first man I ever shot was a big ol' cuss name of Windy Cahill who tried to take his pleasure with me. I got my gun out while he was straddling me on a barroom floor and popped him right in the guts. You know what he said?"

Albert and me shook our collective heads.

"Ooof! That's all he said and bled out like a stuck hog."

This Billy said with something akin to perverse pleasure I thought—coldly and darkly.

Neither Albert nor me said anything to that. What was there to say? Like when he described what Indians would do to you. Made your skin crawl.

Billy soon changed the subject and proceeded to tell us about this place he was from, Lincoln County, down in New Mexico Territory he said. How they had a war going on down there and he almost got killed half a dozen times and several of his friends *had* been killed by what he called the most dogged lawman he'd ever seen.

"Locals call him Lengthy. Killed about everyone he could without an ounce of compunction."

Albert glanced at me.

"Means a feeling of guilt or moral scruple," I said.

"Oh," Albert said. "I figured it was something like that."

"You strike me as right smart, for a darkie, Ivory," Billy said. "I never known no colored folks very personal, unless you count *Mescans* and half-breed Indians as colored. You seem just like a white person, the way you think and act and everything. Fact is, I'm proud to have made your acquaintance."

Well, I didn't appreciate such a left-handed compliment. To me, I was just a person like every other person. What difference did it make what color I was? Of course, I admit, I was seeing it from the inside out, not the other way around. And I'm ashamed to say when I hear the word "Chinaman" a certain image comes to mind.

"Me and Ivory have been friends since we met, ain't that so, Ivory?" Albert said as though to jump to my defense. "He's just like me. I just see Ivory, I don't see no colored."

"Well, it's hard to find good friends you can count on, 'specially in a pinch," Billy said. "No, sir. Good friends who will stick by you through thick and thin is rare indeed. Me, I'm a tried and true friend to them I like, such as the two of you. You can always count on ol' Billy in a pinch."

He no sooner spoke those words then all of a sudden, the evening air was full of whoops and screams as riders came charging forth from a copse of trees off to our left. I about jumped out of my skin. It was a bunch of screaming, charging Indians on thudding horses charging down toward us.

"Injins!" Billy shouted and ran and jumped on his horse bareback, not even bothering with a saddle.

"Run, boys! Every man for himself! Don't let them redskins get holt of you!"

And just as quick as anything I ever saw, he was gone.

"Let's beat feet, Albert!" I shouted. But Albert was already up and running alongside me.

We made our mounts wearing nothing more than our still-damp shirts and trousers, but barely jumped aboard the nervous horses before something whistled past our heads and I thought it a bullet until I realized it made no sound. Arrow. Then several more of them whistled past us.

"Ouch!" Albert shouted as we kicked our horses into a full run. I think they were as afraid of the Indians as we were. I wouldn't know why a horse would know fear same as a human, but they sure seemed like they did. Maybe it was just all the hullabaloo of a sudden that confused them like it did Albert and me.

Darkness was descending fast around us, and we rode into that black wall straight ahead, me praying and hoping we wasn't going to ride straight off an unseen cliff, for we'd come across some earlier that day. Billy had explained in his discourse on the ways of Indians that it was their habit to run buffalo off cliffs where they'd crash on the rocks below and be easy pickings. I sure didn't want to end up easy pickings and I know Albert didn't, either. So, I just held onto the mane of my mount with both fists and hoped for the best.

We got way into the dark and after several miles I told Albert to hold up so's we could listen and maybe figure out if we was still being chased. We'd got in among some trees.

We could hear distant voices, grunts, and guttural sounds, but they came from some distance off in the direction we'd just rode from.

"The camp," Albert whispered. "We left everything including our saddles and boots and dang new Stetson hats."

"Don't forget the pack mule," I whispered back.

"Buster," Albert said.

"Buster?" I said.

"I named him Buster and I sure hope they don't eat poor Buster, he's been a right good mule. Never gave us an ounce of problems."

"Oh, and them sateen shirts we should never have bought in the first place. Made us look like fannies," I said, remembering what Billy had said.

"All we got is these old ones all warshed out of color."

"Hesh," I cautioned. "Sound carries a long ways at night."

"You hesh too, then."

So, I heshed and so did Albert and we listened, then quietly crept off into the darker night still walking our horses and dressed in naught but our warshed-out shirts and warshed-out blue jeans. No hats, no boots, no guns. After we'd gone what we figured was a safe distance and dismounted to let the poor horses catch a blow, Albert said, "Where do you think Billy might have gone?"

"To hell I hope, for abandoning us after all that high talk about the attributes of friendship. Ha!"

"The what of having good friends?" Albert said.

I was in no mood just then to explain another dang word. I heard Albert suck in his breath.

"One of those arrows tore through my leg skin just below my hind end," he said. "I'm bleeding."

"Bad?"

"Nah, not real bad, I reckon. But somewhat bad."

"Make up your mind. Is it bad enough so's you might lose your leg or bleed to death?"

"Nah, it ain't that bad. But if you've ever been smited by an arrow, you'd know how much it hurts."

"Smited?"

"You're not the only one who knows special words," he said.

"You're right," I said. "Now let's keep going. Case them Indians is creeping up on us. They can be real stealthy, remember what Billy said."

"Well, they sure wasn't real stealthy when they rushed our camp. And damn anything Billy said, and for abandoning us."

"What's done is done," I said. But the truth was, Billy abandoning us and saving his own skin without a care to our well-being only proved what I'd suspected about him.

"You're right, Albert. No use crying over spilled milk."

"Water under the bridge," Albert said.

"A bird in the hand is worth two in the bush."

"A stitch in time saves nine."

"What? That don't have anything to do with anything."

"Well, I couldn't think of no more good sayings," Albert said. "It's what my ma used to always say."

We walked and rode our mounts all night and rested up in the day, then rode and walked all night again until we reached the far end of the woods where it opened up into just rocks and tall pine trees and we set down to rest horse and humans alike. Figured if we hadn't been staked out yet and had our eyelids cut off and honey poured over us to attract ants, and that other thing Billy talked about, it might be safe to rest. We dozed some and awoke some until the sky eventually went from black to cat-fur gray.

"What's that yonder?" Albert pointed way off in the distance and down below where it looked like a couple of stars had fallen from the heavens and shimmered in the morning haze.

"Lights, it looks like," I said.

"Well, that's a relief. Maybe we can find us shelter and something to eat."

"Maybe something to wear too, my feet are about all tore up."

"You always did have delicate appendages," Albert said, just to show off his learning word skills and to be cruel, I think.

Well, by the time we worked our way down there, it turned out not to be a house but a town of sorts, along a crooked gulch, both sides, shacks and shanties and pitched tents all looking like barnacles on a ship's hull what with the hills on both sides rising up from the gulch. The only street leading in and out was just a bunch of mud with trash everywhere. Hardly nobody was up and moving about. But the lights we'd seen came from the second floor of a building on the other side of where we'd halted. So, we crossed over, high stepping through mud and animal waste, and knocked on the red door. Then we knocked again until a woman's voice shouted from the other side: "Hold your dang horses."

Well, we are holding 'em, I wanted to shout back, but I was too tired to do so.

"Speaking of such," Albert said, "what *will* we do about our horses? We got no way to even tie 'em off."

It was true; we'd not only run off without our saddles but without tack too.

"Hold 'em, like she said," I muttered.

Finally, the door opened and standing before us was a giant of a woman wearing a gaudy wrapper that barely contained all of her, especially the upper halves that poked out like the bottoms of two babies. I knew what wrappers were because I'd once in a while spy one of the nuns late at night heading to the privy wearing them. But it was no mistaking this woman for a nun.

Sprigs of her platinum hair were tied up in strips of cloth all about her head. Her face was large and doughy and without benefit of rouge, which might have helped her looks some. I think she could have made a meal of the two of us had she wanted.

"Well, ain't you boys a bit young to come to a whorehouse at six in the morning? I mean what do you aim to accomplish, anyway?" she said, staring down at our bare feet and bare heads. It was plain we didn't come for what she was suggesting.

Albert was the first to speak up.

"Our encampment was attacked by Indians," he said, pointing back the way we'd come.

"Mercy, get in here quick!" and she grabbed us both in her big fleshy arms and pulled us inside and shut and barred the door. She smelled like a sweaty blacksmith on a hot afternoon— not that I'd know that personal, but what I imagined such might smell like.

"Indians," she said breathlessly. "How many?"

"Didn't stick around long enough to count 'em," I said.

"Besides, it was getting on dark," Albert said.

"Horatio!" she shouted in a booming voice.

In a moment a large black man appeared from down a hallway.

"These boys were attacked by Indians up in the hills."

He glared down at us with sleepy eyes.

"When?" she asked us.

"A few nights back," I said, still staring at this Horatio fellow and wondering if it was even half possible he could have been my scoundrel of a daddy somehow escaped into the wilds, or maybe half hoping he was and half hoping he was not. But just as quickly rejecting the idea, since I had been long led to believe my daddy had either been killed in the war or died a dozen other ways according to accounts I'd heard. Besides, I couldn't conceive that someone so ugly and fierce looking was kin to me, since I considered myself not unattractive, even if I was the only one who thought so.

He looked down at Albert and me, and especially at me, with hooded and brooding eyes that had come fully awake after the word "Indians" was spoken.

"Why, Missus," he said. "You can't believe nothin' these little peckerwoods say. They just wantin' something to eat, a place to lay they heads. Look at 'em."

She looked at us again when he said that.

"Is it true?" she said. "You boys making up tales about Indians because you know the whole gulch here is as nervous as a hog at butchering time."

We shook our heads.

Albert showed her where he'd been cut by the arrow that was meant to kill him. Had to lower his whipcords to show her, and she bent low and looked closely and ran a finger over the cut, then stood.

"Well, it could be an arrow that cut this urchin's haunch meat," she said to the big man.

"Or it could be he jus' was foolin' around and slid down a tree and got a splinter in his rump," Horatio said. I considered him a doubting Thomas who wasn't about to believe us, or anything we had to say.

Then she noticed our bare muddy feet and here we were standing on a fine carpet runner, too.

"Horatio, you go and alert Sheriff Bullock, tell him what these boys told us, and be quick."

"Yes, Missus," the big man said. He had a voice sounded like it was coming out of a cave. Then she called real loud again.

"Perky, get your skinny rump down here!"

The place smelled a lot like she did, sweaty, but mixed in stale cigar smoke and a dull sweetness like dying flowers. There was fancy flocked paper covering the walls and Belgium carpets everywhere, horsehair divans and a burl-wood cabinet with liquor bottles and a staircase with a polished rail leading upstairs. There were wine-colored drapes along the windows and several settees. It was all real nice and I told myself I could get used to living in such a fine place.

In a minute, coming down those stairs, was a thin, pale creature, also wearing a wrapper, but this one was flat as a board up front, no bosoms at all, and didn't have to concern herself with popping out. Her hair was also tied up in little pieces of cloth like the big lady. I thought she looked a little ridiculous, then quickly considered that I was in no position to pass judgment on the looks of others, considering my own poor condition. Sister Mary Virgin had said to me on more than one occasion: "Remember Ivory, judge not that ye shall be judged. What we see as failings in others, we often fail to see in ourselves." She could have told me that fish rode bicycles and I would have listened.

"Perky," the big lady tells the skinny one soon as he stops on the bottom stair, watching Albert and me like we're mangy dogs let into the house. "Take these boys in the back and make them wash their feet and see can you find a pair of old boots back there in that pile of things our customers have left behind in their haste to get home to their wives and children. Then take them into the kitchen and give them something to eat and drink. They look downright starved."

The girl nodded, her pearly lids half closed, and said: "Come'n, y'all," and we followed her down the hallway.

She took us out a back door where a big tub of rainwater set and told us to wash our feet in it and we did, and the water soothed my sore feet so much I didn't want to take them out again. She handed us each a towel to dry them off before taking us back inside and into a kitchen just off the hall. She cut some old bread with a hard crust, then sliced off some meat from a cold ham and poured us two glasses of water that had a tinny taste to it.

"You are some sorry-looking fools," she grunted. "Where'd you two come from?"

So, we told her the short version, that we were from a town called Last Whisky originally, but that we got involved with chasing a killer and possibly his gang and so on and so forth. She set down and propped her elbow on the table and rested her chin in the palm of her hand as she listened, looking as bored as a heathen at a prayer meeting.

We told her about our friend Gus Monroe and how he'd been slain and our reason for being on the scout and how we got lost after our camp was raided, and for a moment she just sat there as if stunned. But then, her eyes popped open of a sudden.

"What?" she cried. "Did you say Gus Monroe is dead?"

"Yes, he is," I said. "As dead as anyone would care to be."

"When, where, how?" She looked as afraid as Albert and I must have looked afraid when those Indians came charging down on our camp.

We told her what we knew, about One-eye Texas Jack killing Gus and robbing the bank and stealing a banker's bride right out from under him, and how we'd run into a fellow named Billy Bonney who was going to help us capture or kill Gus's murderer and get this banker's wife back in order to collect a big reward, get Gus a first-rate funeral like we'd promised him. And the more we talked the more haunted she looked.

She started to cry bitterly.

"What is it?" I asked when she slowed down her wet, slobbering sobbing.

"Gus and me were supposed to get married," she groaned.

Well, I didn't say nothing but she was young enough to be Gus's daughter, maybe even his granddaughter, and maybe she was simply confused. I knew Gus was a rounder who would tell any woman what he thought they wanted to hear to get what he wanted them to give him; perhaps he'd done such with this one. She seemed awfully naïve and a bit dull in the thinking department. But there I go again, setting judgments on folks and I shouldn't.

"Where was it you met Gus?" Albert asked.

She rolled her teary, reddened eyes.

"Where do you think, boyo? Right here at Madam Solstice's House of Pleasure. This is the grandest cathouse in Deadwood Gulch and everybody who is anybody, and a lot of those who ain't, have paid a visit here, including Gus Monroe after Wild Bill recommended it. Me and Gus fell in love right off. Spent three whole days and nights together. He promised me soon as he got back this way, we'd marry."

Then she started right back into the waterworks, boohooing into hands that appeared much too large for a girl of her frail and slender build.

As soon as she slowed the sobbing down enough, I asked her where was it Gus was headed last time she'd seen him.

She raised up her tearful face and looked at Albert and me with sore, red eyes.

"That feller you said shot him? Well, that's who Gus was after, Texas Jack something or other," she said. "Said he aimed to kill him on sight, collect the reward on his head, then hang up his guns forever and come back and marry me. Said he would buy us a piece of land of our own and build a house facing the mountains and we'd have a basket of kids. Gus said he'd always wanted children but never stayed in one place long enough to have them, and now he is gone, gone, gone!" she bawled. (Let me just say right here, that I'm sure as much as Gus got around, he probably *did* have little tykes running hither thither and yon by a dozen different gals, though he just might not have known it.)

Boohoo. Boohoo. Then she ran out of the room still crying.

"You believe her?" Albert said.

"You mean that Gus wanted to marry her and settle down?" I said.

"No, I mean about Gus being after One-eye Texas Jack? Maybe it's the reason One-eye doused his lights first?"

"It's right possible," I said. "But on the other hand, I don't think from what we know of One-eye, he'd need a reason to kill anybody, Gus included. Such a man that would snatch up a bride from her wedding day and carry her off, I imagine he's capable of most everything."

"You're probably right. But this gal seems awfully sincere and broken up over Gus's death," Albert said.

"Well, maybe Gus was getting soft in his old age and decided that it *was* time to set down roots, and who better to set them down with than a young honey he could plant his man seed in and have fun doing it?" I said.

"That would be Gus," Albert said, flushing red from my bold talk.

About that time, we heard voices out in the hall; then they got closer until they were right in the room with us. Madam

Solstice and her colored man, Horatio, were with another fellow with thick sandy moustaches, a man of whom it could be said had more hair on his upper lip than most men did on their heads. A star was pinned to his coat. He was tall and lean with a no-nonsense gaze.

"I'm Sheriff Bullock," he pronounced. "Madam tells me you boys were attacked by Indians?"

Albert and me nodded.

"Up in the Black Hills? How far from here?"

"A few days back," I said. "We was traveling hard as near possible night and day afterward to get this far. You could say we were lost in our fright to get away and was just lucky to find this here place."

His steel-eyed gaze fell to me, then to Albert.

"You get any of 'em?"

We shook our heads.

"We barely got away with our scalps, the clothes on our backs, and, luckily, our mounts," Albert said a bit dramatically. "We ran one way and Billy took off another. Not sure if they got him or not."

"Billy?"

"Billy Bonney," I said. "He'd been traveling with us."

This popped open the shades of the lawman's eyes.

"Billy the Kid?"

"He didn't call himself that but said others did. Just said his true name was Billy Bonney."

He snorted and sniggered.

"Solstice, I'm afraid these urchins have snookered you."

"How do you know, Mr. Bullock?" she said.

"Why Garrett killed that kid last July. Unless he's a ghost." Then he sniggered some more and said he was going back to bed on account of he had to help out at the hardware store, that his partner, Sol, was taking the afternoon off to get married.

Soon as he left out, Madam glared at us.

"Why didn't you just tell me the truth, I would have fed you. You didn't need to lie and get this whole camp riled up. If it was to get around that there was an Indian attack, everybody would be in a frenzy."

"We weren't lying," I said.

For a moment she stood staring me down. Horatio still had them sleepy eyes but he didn't look upset.

"Perky, stop that damn caterwauling," Madam shouted at the girl. "What ever are you carrying on about, child?"

"Oh, Miz Solstice, Gus is dead."

"Who the hell is Gus?"

This set the girl to even more sobbing and blubbering.

"Well, we best get on," I said." and Albert nodded. "We are truly sorry to raise a ruckus, but every word of what we said was the truth—about the Indians, and Billy and all the rest. Why else do you figure we'd run around bootless?" For I was a bit put out that the sheriff or she did not believe us and was ready to shake the dust from my feet.

"Probably wise," Madam Solstice said. She didn't try and talk us out of it, which is the same as telling us to get out. And so we did.

Once outside a fellow on a charging horse holding a severed head by its long hair went racing past.

"Say," Albert said, "what's with all these fellows running around with cut heads anyway?"

I shrugged.

"Beats me, though it does seem somewhat odd."

Morning had fallen halfway into the gulch and Albert and me were no longer the only ones out on the street. The sound of hammering all over town was like pistol shots. Hammering and sawing and cussing filled the air. The whole place looked a shambles now that we saw it in better light; everything in a state of disorder with plenty of wagons hauling sawn lumber and miners with picks over their shoulders and pipes poking out of their grizzled maws. Men drunkenly fought in the street and it was not yet breakfast time.

And as a final insult—we saw that our horses were no longer standing out front, and nowhere up or down the muddy street, either.

"Somebody stole our mounts," I complained.

"We sure got ourselves into a pickle, Ivory," Albert said.

Albert looked, for the first time since news of his pap's murder, as forlorn as I've ever seen him.

"Whatever are we going to do, Ivory?"

"I think it's time we paid back measure for measure," I said.

"Meaning?"

"That's the part I ain't quite concluded," I said.

"You better get to concluding it."

"Believe me, I am."

Just then the door opened and Horatio was looming over us like a black storm cloud, like a curse or plague of death about to put us asunder.

"How come you all ain't skedaddled on away from here?" he said in that cave-like voice.

"Somebody pinched our horses and we was just considering our next move," I said.

He looked like he didn't even believe us about the horses.

"Perky in yonder was tellin' me what you all told her."

"Well, that depends," I said, unsure of his interest in what we told that poor weeping girl.

"Is it true, about you all aiming to catch this fellow what stole a banker's wife and collect a *re*-ward?"

"True enough," I said, "but it seems like the gods are against us."

He looked heavenward, then dropped that brooding glare

back down on us.

"What gods you talkin' about? Ain't no God against you. Why you speak blasphemy?"

So I quickly explained that it was just an expression of old, though even then I was not sure he understood.

He glanced back over his shoulder at the red door as if to make sure nobody was listening.

"You boys think you know where this fool is at—the one killed Perky's feller and got the big reward on him?"

"Could be," I said.

"What's the name?"

"I'm sorry, Mr. Horatio," Albert said. "But we're in dire straits here and we're not about to be cut out of that reward money. We need it to bury a good friend and compatriot of ours—otherwise he might become . . . what's the word, Ivory?"

I am not sure exactly what word Albert was thinking of, so I imagined my own and said, "desiccated," then quickly added: "Dried up, like old leaves or dead cicadas."

I noticed how big Horatio's hands were when he squeezed them into fists. I figured he ever hit you with one, that'd be it, so long and bar the door, Katy. He scared me more than just a little. Way more than Rufus Buck ever had. Well, maybe not way more, but just as much.

"I don't know nothin' about no dessycation or what all, but I'll tell you all somethin'," he said. "Let me thows in wit you and I'll hep you out. I never met any man I can't whup."

"It's a dangerous mission," said Albert. I knew he was trying to make excuses to avoid the big man coming along without insulting him. Albert might not always be the brightest light in a room, but he learns quick and I think he learned about taking on partners after Billy ran off on us.

"Danger's my middle name," Horatio said. "I ain't scared a' nothin'. I was in the war, got shot four times. Dint kill me.

Nothin' can. Witchy woman predicted it. Said, 'Horatio, you gone live a long life. Bullets come you way and sees who they aimin' at, they just turn right aroun' an' go back into the gun.'"

"How do we know when we catch up with One-eye Texas Jack, you won't kill us and claim the reward?" I said.

The he turned that frightful stare on me, the whites of his eye shot through with what looked like tiny red worms in milk, the breathing coming through his nose sounding like sighs.

"On 'count I a Christian man. My mama raised me right. I don't smoke or drink or . . ." He paused and looked back at the door again. ". . . any them other things mostly, but maybe one or two now and again. Flesh and blood needs flesh and blood, you know what I means?"

"But you killed men in the war," said Albert, "and don't the Bible say, 'Thou shall not kill?'"

I wish he hadn't challenged Horatio, for who knew what might set him off?

"War a different kinda killin,' and don't count." Then Horatio stuck out one of his large palms and spit in it and said, "On my word, we shake."

Albert just stood there for a moment, then spit in his hand and shook Horatio's and his white paw disappeared for a moment. Then Horatio turned to me and spit in his hand again and stuck it out. So, I did the same, but not because I wanted to shake a hand with spit in it, I was just too afraid not to.

"There, thas my word, Lord strike me dead if I'm lyin'." And he rolled his eyes heavenward again, saying as he did: "Horatio only gots one God, not a bunch like you all."

There was no way then to get out of our bargain.

"I'll get you shoes fer yer feet and some hats fer yer heads. Guns. I'll get you guns and bullets too. Then we can go."

"Well, that would sure enough show good faith," I said. "Go in with our shooting irons and ill intentions blazing away." I said, being overly dramatic.

His grin was whitely toothsome.

"I likes the sound of that," he said.

"Billy told us he had done some powerful gun work himself and the only way to defeat your adversary was with overwhelming force and surprise," I said.

"Well how's the two of yous supposed to pull that off?"

"Don't know, Billy never said how," Albert said.

"Don't know too much," said Horatio. "But I do know that all this country here"—he then flung out an arm the size of a log—"is plumb full of dangerous men such as this Blind-Eye Texan Jack. Thas why it better to have a man like me along. You know what this feller look like 'sides havin' a blind eye? How we supposed to find him?" Horatio said.

I didn't take the wanted poster with Texas Jack's picture on it from my money pouch underneath my shirt. It was the one thing we hadn't left behind at the camp when attacked by the Indians.

"We sorta know what he looks like," I lied before Albert could blurt out more information.

"I lissnin,' " Horatio said, his eyes already growing greedy.

"Ugly," I said. "He's real ugly, 'bout like the hind end of a mule, got a big long scar from ear to cheek. Can't be too many running around looking like him."

Albert picked up the ruse.

"Besides, I reckon a man of his reputation won't be that hard to find once we get down to Robbers Roost," Albert said boldly. "If he's down around there, ought to be folks who know of him could . . ." Suddenly Albert knew he might have given away too much information by divulging the fact of Robbers Roost being One-eye's hideout.

"Thas' where you reckon he is, this Robbers Roost?"

"Maybe," I quickly said. "Not one hundred percent certain,

it was just a name we heard was possible, one of several. More likely he could be in Missouri hanging out with the James boys." It was the only other thing I could come up with.

That seemed to satisfy Horatio. He didn't look like he had gone too far in school, maybe less far than me. And if the nuns hadn't beat a good education into me, Horatio probably would have been smarter than me, no doubt. For even a complete fool could figure out how fast I was retreating and making a story.

"Well, then, I'll go wit you and my guns blazin' too," Horatio said. "They's a stage leaving in two days heading south, all the way to Cheyenne and if'n this Robbers Roost is along the way, we'll find it, sure 'nuff. Come'n, follow me."

So, we followed behind his lumbering figure, other men stepping aside for him even if they had to step into the street. We reached the end of the block and he said we'd take a shortcut and we turned up a trash-strewn alley. Several cats hissed atop garbage piles as we passed and it reminded me of a bad dream I had once, for I was never comfortable around those feline creatures. I always found them to be spooky the way they'd sneak up on you and clamp onto your leg with their sharp claws for no reason other than they were plain spiteful.

The alley smelled terrible, and when we got near to the end, there was a man lying in the garbage, his mouth agape, but I couldn't tell if he was alive or dead. Horatio didn't even pay attention to him but rounded the corner where a row of small shanties stood, some of them with ladies' underthings hanging on rope lines.

Horatio stopped in front of one of them and called out, "Sunflower!" Then he looked back at us and for the first time, I saw him smile and he had not one, but two gold teeth, one upper and one lower. I never saw anybody with gold teeth. Horatio was proving to be an interesting character, but I wasn't sure I wanted to know too much more about him.

"Sunflower!" he shouted again. "Get yo behind out heah!"

Then the door to one of the shanties opened to reveal a pert gal of warm cocoa color and it filled me with a nice satisfaction and comfort to see there was another Negro around. Hanging off her bony frame was a faded sack dress. She was barefooted and had large liquor-colored eyes.

"You gone keep these heah boys till I comes fer 'em," Horatio said.

"Why you gonna do me that way, Horatio?" Sunflower whined. "How I gone make any money with these two fools hangin' round."

"Don't you fret none, honey,' Horatio said. "I take care of you, make up for it, okay? Now let 'em in and you watch over 'em till I gets back. And when I do, I bring you a little somethin' fer yer troubles, okay?"

She looked at Albert, then at me, like we were the plague coming to wipe her out.

"All right," she said sounding defeated, "but only two days, Horatio, you lissenin?"

He turned and waved a hand over his head, then was gone.

She stood with her hands on her hips still looking at us.

"Well, you two fools coming in or ain't you?"

It was terribly small and cramped inside with just room enough for a single bed up against one wall; a little woodstove at the back; a bucket along the other wall with a shelf of dry goods, coffee, flour, sugar, cans of beans, and potted meat; and a trunk at the foot of the bed. It was dim and hard to see until she went over and lighted an oil lamp that filled the room with greasy yellow light.

"I got no place for you to sit but on the floor," she said. "You fools want coffee? I'ma fix myself some."

"Yes'm," Albert and me said in unison.

I bet she couldn't weigh more than seventy pounds soaking

wet, but it was a bit hard to tell because that sack dress pretty much covered up everything but her arms and the bottom of her legs and feet.

Me and Albert didn't say anything until she finished fixing the coffee and handed us each a cup, then poured herself one.

"I'ma be outside," she said then and stepped out the door and closed it behind her.

"What do you think?" Albert said.

"I think right now things could be worse," I said.

He looked toward the door.

"I reckon's you might see it that way," he said with an impish grin.

"Say what?" I said.

"You know what I'm talking about, Ivory, don't think I didn't see how you looked at that gal."

"Folderol," I said.

"That's the best you can come back with, Ivory?"

"I reckon for now it is."

"I think we should keep our thoughts on going after the reward, don't you?"

"You're right," I said.

"Still, we're in a fix what with no boots or hats or guns or horses, out here in the middle of nowhere with folks we don't know," Albert said. "Don't you worry?"

"Sure," I said. "I worry. I worry mostly about eating instead of going hungry and getting my rest."

"That all you worry about?"

I could tell Albert was as uncomfortable as I've ever known him, us thrown in with strangers.

"I worry about us getting our heads lopped off and having some crazy man riding up and down the street with it," Albert said.

"Don't let that fool get to you," I said. "We might have just been imagining that on account of we saw the same thing before, remember?"

"It's a sign, I think?" Albert said.

"A sign some folks can be as crazy as a privy rat," I said. "I don't believe our time is up yet, Albert. But, if so, I want you to know you're the best friend I ever made. Wasn't it you who told me that time that everything that happens under the sun was long ago writ by the finger of God, that our fortunes are foretold, you and me and everyone's and I don't think the Lord would kill you off just yet." Of course, I didn't necessarily believe it, but I was trying to ally Albert's fears.

I had to think a second to come up with a reasonable answer that a smart boy like Albert would believe. So, I thought, and thought, but my thoughts kept wandering to the skinny colored gal and I was having a hard time concentrating for argument's sake.

"Okay, I'll tell you, why, Albert."

"I'm listening."

"On account of you have never been with a girl before, have you?"

"Of course, I have. Me and Sally Beth was sweethearts, remember."

"No, I don't mean sparking," I said. "I mean in that other way, you know."

He gave me that quizzical look only he could give, all full of curiosity and stupidity when he didn't know what I was talking about. And then suddenly those selfsame eyes found the answer.

"Oh, you mean . . . ?"

I nodded.

He blushed.

"No, Ivory, Sally Beth's not like that, she's completely innocent."

"I figured she was," I said. "And that's why I don't think He would take you until you've done it with a gal."

Then his eyes narrowed on me like a gunfighter about to kill you with his quick draw.

"Oh, and I suppose you have," he said accusingly.

"Well, let's just say that if the Lord calls me, I'm qualified to go." Of course, I added my best grin.

"I don't think being with a gal in that way makes a bit of difference," Albert said after several minutes. "I think that our fates has already been writ and it don't make a lick of sense to have being naked with a gal whether your name is in that book of life or not."

"Hogwash, Albert. I've heard that argument before—back at the orphanage. We had us a real old nun, Sister Abigail, who was not all there, like a cowboy kicked in the head"—I tapped my head—"who spewed such nonsense. I mean do you know how much time it would take to write down everybody's name on earth since the beginning of time? No, sir, I don't buy it."

"Well, how do you explain it, then?"

"How do I explain what, that we're cooped in a skinny whore's crib like a pair of roosters waiting for the butcher to lop off our heads?"

"Please don't say that about getting our heads lopped off," he said.

"I don't explain it, Albert, it is what it just is, circumstance and misfortune. I reckon we just choose to do whatever it is we do," I said. "While those nuns were rapping my knuckles, the old priest that was there told us God gave us free will, meaning we can do whatever we want. But if we screw up, well, too bad for us. And I reckon we done screwed up."

Before we knew it, we stretched out on the floor and fell dead asleep only to be awakened some time later by the girl, Sunflower, dropping two pairs of boots next to us and a pair of dirty flop hats not nearly as nice as the new Stetsons we lost in the Indian raid. Why, I could just see a couple of those heathens riding about and showing off their new hats.

"Horatio brung you these," she said "You fools sleeping like dogs, you know it? Anybody walk by, they'd think I keep a pack of bulldogs snorin' in heah."

In spite of her harsh mouth, she had a pretty smile, I had to give her that.

"I worked it out with Flossie next door," she said. "One of you all can sleep there tonight. She out of commission, anyway, for the night."

I noticed how she kept her gaze on me and wondered if it was because we were both colored. I wanted to ask her what she meant by this Flossie person being out of commission but decided to not ask any questions.

We pulled on our boots.

"Could have used socks," I said.

"Yas, and I could use me a fine rich man to carry me off to San Francisco too."

"Well now what? Which one of us has to stay with Flossie?" asked Albert.

"Who you think?" she said. "You get on over to Flossie's— she expecting you."

"Me?"

Sunflower shook her head and went to the door and went out and came back in a minute.

"It okay, Flossie's back from the privy."

And she practically pushed Albert out the door, then pointed to the shanty he was supposed to go to.

"I'll see you later, I guess," Albert said as he disappeared into the shanty.

"You hungry, fool?" she said to me. "Cook you up some of this potted meat and beans if you is."

"I can eat," I said.

She looked me over top to bottom.

"I just bet you can."

She cooked outside in a communal iron kettle it looked like and we ate on tin plates sitting on the side of her bed, and in spite of everything, it was good eating too. I reckon I was starved about halfway or better so that might have made it taste good. She sat close to me so that our arms touched as we ate. It gave me a real good feeling.

After we finished, she took the plates outside and must have washed them for they were clean when she returned. Then she sat down with a sack of Bull Durham and some smoking papers and rolled herself a cigarette and I watched her lick the edge of the paper with the delicate tip of her pink tongue before rolling the paper over and twisting off the ends.

"You smoke?" she said.

I shook my head.

"It's bad for you," I said.

"Lots of things is bad for you," she said, striking a kitchen match to light the cigarette. I saw how the flame jumped up into those liquid brown eyes and that did something to me I can't rightly explain.

I watched her smoke, with one thin leg crossed over the other, and was entranced like I was the snake and she the charmer. I'd read in a book there were actually men in India who charmed poisonous snakes they kept in baskets by blowing a flute. I thought of watching Sunflower smoking that cigarette like it was a flute and she was charming me and I sure didn't fight the feeling, either.

She stood and went to the little stove and opened the door and tossed the cigarette in once she had smoked it down about as far as she could, then came back and stretched before me and looked down at me.

"You ever been with a girl, Ivory?" she said.

I nodded.

"You never did!" she protested.

"Once," I said. "Had a girlfriend."

"Well, does you still got her?"

"No, long gone. What about you?" I say.

"Me? I don't got no girlfriend. What you think I am, fool?"

She laughed like I was tickling her or something.

"No, I mean, do you have a beau somewhere?"

She laughed even more.

"Gals like me got lots of beaus," she said. "Every night. Fact is, you know what they call us?"

I shook my head.

"Brides of the multitudes and I guess we is."

Then she reached up and pulled that sack dress over her head and stood before me in all her natural glory. And I have to say, she looked just like what my imagination of her was, had I of thought on it, which maybe I did, and maybe I didn't. For a thin little gal, she sure was pretty, sleek, and bronze in that little bit of lamplight, with bosoms the sizes of pomegranates with black coin-sized tips. I sucked in my breath and held it in wonder at the sight.

"Well?"

"What?" I say.

"Well, do you like what you see, Ivory?"

"I reckon I don't not like it," I said, for her naked boldness had tied my brain in knots.

"You got two dollars?"

I shook my head.

"Ain't got spit," I said, even though that wasn't true. I still had the money sack tied around my neck and under my shirt but was afraid to show it among strangers, even skinny girl strangers, especially knowing what she was.

"We had to run for our lives when Indians jumped us. Reason

we had no footwear or hats, either. No guns, no saddles, no nothing."

She looked displeased when I told her I had no money and then she put her dress back on and went to acting toward me like I had kicked her mama.

"Well you right about that," she said. "You ain't worth spit. If you'd had some money I could have showed you a right good time. But I'm a working gal, like all these others along this line—crib girls we is. Coloreds and whites and Chinese gals. To a wantin' man, it don't matter what color we is or who we is just as long as we females. Can't everbody work in Madam Solstice's big house, elsewise I'd be over there instead of stuck in this crib. Wasn't that we is cheap, wouldn't no man even come 'round."

Then she pushed me aside and lay on the bed and wrapped herself up in her blankets like a cocoon, snuffling as she did so, leaving me to wonder at her way of life, not understanding how a girl could do what she did but for the fact she had to eat and keep in out of the rain like everbody else.

I stepped outside into the dying light of day, the sky overhead streaked with red fingers across the darker background, the air chilling now that the sun had gone out of it.

I was feeling mighty glum having thought for a moment the way things turned out between Sunflower and me, wondering if maybe I should have paid her the two dollars so I wouldn't feel so lonesome. Then I wondered if maybe I should come back for her when Albert and me finished taking care of One-eye. Maybe take her back to Last Whisky where it was nice and there were churches and good built houses and plenty of land to build us a little cabin and get some horses and raise some crops and get the preacher to marry us and have some babies running around; then slowly, very slowly, we'd get old together and our hair would turn white as cotton and I would die first and then she would die of heartbreak and we'd both get buried in the same section of the little cemetery and not far from where Albert and his wife was to be buried and his pa and ma too.

"Ivory?"

"What?"

"Ivory?"

It was Albert whispering to me in the gloaming.

"What is it?" I whisper back.

"That gal in there asked me for three dollars to get in the bed with her."

"Mine asked for two."

"But have you seen Flossie?" he said with a jerk of his head toward the cabin he stood in front of.

"No."

"Well, if you had, she should be the one paying *me* three dollars. Homely as our pack mule, Buster, that the Indians stole."

I sighed heavily.

"I got a bad feeling about all this," I say.

"Me too," he said coming closer. "I have a sense of doom somehow."

"I think it's time to take charge of our destiny and not let it be writ by the hand of the Lord," I said. " 'Sides, this hour, he's probably tuckered out anyway and we'd be helping him to get his rest."

Albert didn't say anything in rebuttal. I think he was still too stunned from his experience with Flossie. And then a storm kicked up out of nowhere. I mean thunder and lightning and rain like you wouldn't believe, the raindrops the size of nickels, and as cold and hard so's it knocked down the brims of our new old hats Horatio had brought, causing us to tip our heads back to see.

"Well, Lord!" Albert said. "If it could get worse, I'd like to see it."

"Don't tempt the maker," I said.

While the rain fell, we slunk off back toward the town itself, as if it could be called a town. To me, it looked like a long, crooked ditch with people spilled into it from the saloons and cathouses like the rain itself. Shacks and tents all jammed together like crooked teeth in a poor man's mouth.

The rain boiled up on the ground and fell slantwise on account of the wind funneling down through the gulch so's we had to hold our wet hats on our heads to keep them from blowing clean away.

But the storm didn't seem to bother anybody else in the gulch that night, for the saloons, which was about every other door, kept right on with their revelry of folks laughing and cussing and staggering out and falling face flat into the mud where they lay still as dead men. And every once in a while, there was gunfire to keep up competition with the storm's thunder.

We saw a pair of saddle horses as wet and miserable as we felt, tied up out front of one place—the Number 10, according to the name painted along its door jamb. One of the horses was a gray and the other a black.

"It's destiny," I said to Albert.

"What is?" he shouted over the storm's roar.

"Them two horses. Like they're just waiting for somebody with a compassionate heart to come along and relieve them of their misery."

"What?"

So, this time I shouted louder.

"Does them two horses look like they want to be standing out there? Just look at 'em."

I grabbed Albert by the arm and led him over to the nags.

"You get on that one, and I'll take this one," I said climbing aboard the black; it just seemed like a good match, that colored horse and me and the gray one for Albert, for he was looking a bit peaked and gray himself.

Albert stood, looking up at me.

"What are you doing?" he shouted.

"What's it look like?" I shouted back.

"Stealing horses is what it looks like, but tell me that we're not. We could get hanged for this," he shouted, holding his hat brim up with one hand.

"Damn right, so you better come on."

Next I know, we're riding hell-bent for leather out of that place so hard mud was flying and stinging rain was lashing our faces as if we was running through nettles and briars.

Horse thieves. That's what we'd become, all in the name of doing the right thing by ol' Gus, who had himself probably did a few bad things for the sake of doing good. Or, maybe not.

CHAPTER 4

We were still riding, half asleep in the saddle, when dawn broke over the Black Hills and you'd a thought we were in a different world than the one the night before.

We finally led our purloined ponies down into some pines and slid off to lie down on a bed of pine needles, tying the reins of the horses to our wrists to keep them from running off. We might have been just ignorant boys, but fool us once, and shame on us, fool us twice and shame on faithless horses.

"I feel rode wet and put away hard," Albert said.

"I think that's rode hard," I said, "and surely we are, put away wet, I mean."

Then we slept like a pair of whipped hounds.

I dreamt of smelling bacon cooking and the dark scent of woodsmoke and angels singing, when my eyes popped open like they'll do when Jesus feels you've slept enough and ought to be doing something other, or have entered some sort of shameless heaven.

And sure enough, I wasn't dreaming, it was right there before me, the source of my awakening disturbance.

A woman dressed in greasy buckskins squatted by the fire singing softly. At least I gauged her as a woman by the high sound of her voice, for she could as easily have been a man, seeing only the back of her, the wide haunches and short cropped hair.

She must have heard me sit up, for she turned around and

looked at me and I've never before or since seen such a homely woman. She smiled around her cigarette.

"Well, hello, sweetness," she said.

I could only nod.

"You'n that other pilgrim there I thought at first to be dead, killed by redskins, which is not all that uncommon around these parts if you know what I mean? My horse, Jimbo, yonder, smelt your two broomtails and drew me here, otherwise I'd still been riding along the road purty as you please. Lucky I found you urchins, otherwise who knows the outcome of your fates."

I shook Albert half awake and he muttered and tried to knock my hand away. "Leave me be, Ivory . . ."

The woman removed her smoke, looked at it, spat off to the side, and continued to eyeball me and Albert like we was breakfast victuals she planned on eating along with that bacon.

"So, your handle is Ivory, is it, and his is what?" she said.

"That's Albert, my pal," I said, trying my best to seem a little older than I was. Pals is a word that means something out in this country.

"Albert and Ivory," she said in a singsong way. "Ivory and Albert. Well, ain't you a pair of doodles. This bacon's almost done and I got biscuits rising in the Dutch oven and we'll be eatin' like shoat hogs here in a minute."

"Mind I ask who *you* are?" I said.

"Sonny boy, you just met Wild Bill Hickok's widow. Name's Calamity Jane Hickok, I reckon you've heard of me, now, ain't you? Poor Bill . . ." She started in sobbing but I did not see any tears coming out of her eyes, but the rest of her sorrow seemed genuine, though I mostly had my thoughts on those biscuits and that bacon.

"Poor William," said she, snorting the snot back up her beaky nose. "A dirty cross-eyed coward gunned him down the very day I was off to the fort taking care of sick soldiers. Time I got back, they had my dear husband planted in the cemetery up on Mount Moriah as if my feelings where he should be laid to rest didn't matter a spit—me, his own dear wife. 'Scuse me, I got a sudden need and got to go in the weed, can you watch this bacon a second?"

Without waiting for an answer, she stood up and hurried off to just beyond some further trees. I went over to the cook fire and forked over the bacon, looked around, then fished a strip out and nibbled on it. My poor belly felt bereft at not having tasted food the last dozen hours.

Finally, Albert sat up, knuckling the last of sleep out of his eyes.

"Where the heck'd you get that bacon, Ivory?"

"Ain't mine, it's hers," I said, pointing toward where she went in among the trees. He looked around.

"What in the world are you talking about?"

I started to answer when she came forth buttoning up the front of her pants.

"Well, I see you ain't dead, neither," she said. "Glad to make yer acquaintance. "I'm the widder Hickok."

"Huh?"

She looked at me as she squatted down by the fire and took a rag out of her back pocket to lift the lid off the Dutch oven.

"Is he all right?" she asked me. "He acts like a mush brain."

"Mostly he is," I said unable to keep from grinning. Albert gave me a cruel look.

"How did you get here?" he asked the widder.

"Why, same as you, my hoss, Jimbo, yonder, named him after my late husband who was all over famous until some low dog skunk murdered him." A little ways off, cropping grass, was the big spotted horse with a fancy Mexican saddle.

"Oh, Jimbo's a looker, ain't he?" she said. "I prefer my men and animals to be handsome. I think these victuals is about ready to eat."

"I thought you said you were married to Bill Hickok?" I said, for I am a stickler for detail.

"Oh, well, Bill is what they called him, but his true name was Jim. So that's what I named that'n after. Dig in."

So, we did, putting bacon on biscuits, and I have to tell you it was delicious, and as we ate away, she told us her Christian name was Martha Jane Canary.

"I go by the name of Calamity," she explained, licking the grease from her fingers, then swiping them on the seat of her buckskin pants. " 'Count of folks give me that name. You know you made your bones when folks give you a nickname. Out here, half the folks worth spit has a nickname. Even that low dog what killed my husband, Jack McCall, who was hisself called Crooked Nose Jack right up till the day he was dropped through the trap and jerked to Jesus. Hanged him over in Yankton where they is civilized folks. Served him right too. I wished I'd been there to fill his corpse full of lead from my pistols."

She said all this in a jocular way, and not distressed at all like you'd think a widder would be. Heck I never even knew that the great Wild Bill was married and was a little taken aback at his choice of a bride now that I had got a gander at her. But then, the West had a shortage of women and so a lot of men take what they can get and I reckon Bill Hickok was no different in that regard. Then, too, it could have been all the liquor he drank might have had an effect over his judgment. Seemed I'd read in *Harper's Weekly* an article that said Wild Bill was suffering from eye problems just before he died. Well, looking at the widder, I sure didn't doubt that maybe it was true.

Swallowing a cup of coffee, Jane said, "Why heck, you'd be shocked at the number of proposals for marriage I've gotten, before and since Bill's demise. Even had one feller offer me a sailing ship if I'd marry him. I says now where in blue blazes am I to sail a ship out here in these wilds? 'Sides, he was already married, or I just might have taken him up on it, but unlike some, I've got morals."

At this, she roared with laughter and slapped her knee two or three times.

"So, where is it you two orphans is off to?" she asked.

"We're on the hunt for a killer," Albert piped up, I think mostly to confirm to Jane he was no mush head.

"Oh?"

"One-eye Texas Jack Crowfoot, you ever heard of him?"

She rolled one eye and then the other in deducing whether she had or had not heard of Texas Jack.

"Well, I did know of a Texas Jack," she said, "but his last name was Omohundro, could it be him, this feller you're seeking out? He was a real swell feller too. Went with my Bill and Cody all the way east to star in stage plays. I wouldn't think he'd turn to murder. Though, with men, you just never know what they might turn to. Why, I've seen preachers' wives with black eyes."

So, I carefully reached in under my shirt and dug out the wanted poster and showed it to her. She brayed like a mule.

"Oh, lord, no! 'At feller wouldn't make a pimple on the other Jack's behind. Sorry, boys, can't help you with that one, wished I could."

"He killed a good friend of ours much the same as your husband, murdered."

I had to jump in.

"And stole a banker's wife."

"Waugh! Now that sounds like the worst sort of four flusher. You reckon him to be in Deadwood? Is that where you're headed? I'm going there my ownself. Heck, I'll help you string him up!"

"No," I said, "we just came from there last night."

She looked off in the direction where Deadwood lay.

"That's surprisin'," she said. "Every low-down scoundrel and murdering son of a buck on two legs is either in or soon to be going to Deadwood. You sure he wasn't there?"

"I'm pretty sure," I said.

Then she stopped and looked over at our pilfered mounts.

"Why, that one looks like Barney Offal's cayuse?" she said of the black gelding.

"No, ma'am, that's my horse, I bought him off of Barney. His luck was running poor at the poker table," I said, grateful for my ability to lie quickly.

The concern left her face and she cackled like a hen being chased by a rooster around the barnyard.

"That Barney features himself a poker player bar none, but he couldn't win a pot if he was playin' against hisself. How much'd you skin him for on that horse, anyway?"

"Twenty dollars," I said.

"Waugh! I'll give you forty for it, double your money?"

"No," I said, "we need these horses to catch our man and bring him to justice and get that poor wife back to the banker."

"Is it a reward in it?"

Albert started to speak but I jumped in first.

"Oh, no, ma'am, we couldn't take any money for doing what's right."

She looked at me with her eyes all squinched like she was disbelieving me, then let out a war hoop.

"You two peckerwoods is either brave or stupid, but God bless you both for being such fine young youths who is doing the right thing. It's harder and harder to come across young folks with good hearts anymore. Seems like all they want to do is start trouble and harass their elders."

I thought she might even cry, but instead she said, "Say, I don't suppose you boys would like to take a turn with me in the blankets before you skin out, would you? Ever since my Bill was murdered, I just have a hankering to be loved up all the time it seems like. Now I don't reckon nobody could top ol' Bill for a lover, and I surely would know, many lovers as I had, and surely wouldn't expect you two little cockers to come close, but hey, a body takes what a body can get, you know, so what's say ye? Who'd like to go first? Give you braggin' rights for some time to come?"

We said we understood that neither of us could possibly compare to Wild Bill in the lovemaking department and we'd only leave her more disappointed and miserable if we was to try, sort of like a man dying of thirst who only gets to drink a single raindrop. However, it didn't seem to deter her much.

"Why I almost feel sinful over feeling so horned up, if you get my drift," she hooted. "But then I stop and think, Well, Jane, ain't it the nature of men and beasts to mate, and ain't it a woman's nature to let 'em? And I answer, of course it is, you see it all the time in the animal kingdom and nobody gives it a second thought. What'll you say? First one then the other, you two can figure out which wants to go first. Unless of course, you would like to both pitch hay together, so to speak."

Her eyes were glistening with anticipation and I was nervously doing some quick thinking because I knew Albert was less experienced at this sort of thing than I was and couldn't have come up with an excuse if it was branded on his forehead, sitting there with his jaw unhinged, so that gnats and small birds and such could just fly right in.

"Jane," I said real boldly. "Poor Albert here promised his mother on her deathbed that he would remain pure until his wedding day, ain't that right, Albert?"

Albert sat almost cross-eyed looking at me, but finally nodded his head.

"Yes'm. I did. And I aim to carry through on that promise,

because, well, she was dying and ain't much worse a fella can do than lie to a dying soul, especially his ma."

"Oh, you sweet creature," she said, almost mournfully, then turned her gaze on me.

"How about you there, Ivory? I only been with two other fellas of color, one was a Mex and the other a chink, so not exactly same as you."

"I surely see it as a fine compliment, Miss Jane, but I caught the pox back yonder in Deadwood, at a place run by a Madam Solstice, and it's making everything difficult. It's a real bad case too. The medico said there was every possibility I might lose the whole dang thing I don't get the cure soon."

She howled like a coyote with a burr in its paw.

"Madam Solstice! Why she claims to run the best house in the gulch and I can't tell you how many fellers has gone blind from catching the pox from there. Why, she's just a high-priced crib gal. I surely feel sorry for you, boyo, I really do. Wished I had gotten to you before you paid that lying old ox a visit."

Well, such talk soured Jane on the idea of rolling around in a blanket with me, and who could blame her after the whoppers we fed her.

"I've had the pox myself a time or two," she commiserated, "and I know it can put a crimp in a body's style and wouldn't want to go through it once more. I was lucky though, I didn't have a pizzle to potentially fall off."

She slapped her knees and stood suddenly.

"Well, since it don't look like we can strike a bargain, I'll be seeing you boys maybe in the far future, maybe not." She cackled, and began packing up her Dutch oven and fry pan and bacon but leaving Albert and me the remaining few biscuits, as if seeing us as charity cases, I supposed. Then she hopped on her Jimbo and rode off with a final "Hidey Ho, children of Ham!"

Albert looked at me and I simply shrugged.

"We best get before she reaches the Gulch and looks up Barney, whose horse we stole, and tells him of our encounter and he comes chasing us with a hanging posse."

"Agreed."

So, once more we fled, this time not from Indians but ugly hankering gals and irate horse owners who might want their nags back and dangle a couple of foolish boyos from a tree limb.

CHAPTER 5

Everything seemed to be going good for about another hour, and then it went suddenly bad.

Stepping out into the road, three disheveled white men pointed guns at us, and if you've ever stared down the barrel of a gun, much less three, then you know the effect it had on Albert and me.

"Hold it right there," one of them snarled, a stumpy little fellow wearing a sparkly vest and striped trousers. And when he talked through a crooked mouth, he exposed crooked teeth laid over each other like a collapsed fence.

"Get down off them nags and surrender your weapons!" he ordered.

"We got none," I said and held my empty hands out.

"Oh, you think I'm gonna fall for that, you little black cuss?" said crooked teeth.

I shrugged.

"Fall for it or not," I said, feeling a little put out for being called a black cuss by this white devil as if he had any right to say such to me when it was him holding the gun and doing the robbing.

"We better do as they say, Ivory," Albert said, sliding down off his stolen horse, which I figure is about to be stolen again if I'm any judge of evil-looking characters with guns. Me and my stolen horse was just getting comfortable with each other and I sure hated the idea we was about to part ways.

A stick-looking fellow holding a shotgun wagged it around and cocked back the rabbit-ear hammers, I suppose to make a point how truly dangerous scatterguns are. Well, if so, he wasted the effort, for just seeing that twin barrel made a point all by its lonesome. I got off my horse quick.

"Take them cayuses, Pegleg," Stumpy said to the third one, who, as he moved I could see had a canted hip and thought of Jane's comment about fellows in the west having nicknames. The one doing the ordering was holding a long-barreled revolver—a Walker Colt maybe—that looked almost too much for him, while his companion limped forward and snatched the reins of our mounts and led them away without so much as a snort or toss of their heads, the faithless beasts.

"Now, empty them pockets, boys," Stumpy ordered.

Me and Albert turned out our pockets.

Nothing.

"Take off them boots and shake 'em out."

We pulled off our boots and shook them out.

Still nothing.

"No guns and no money," moaned Stumpy. "Just these horses. I ought to shoot you boys for being so dang poor. Practically useless, the way I see it. No right to take up good air."

"You're right, mister," I said, "even though you'd just be wasting precious bullets if you shot Albert and me. Why death would practically be a blessing after what all we been through."

Stupid men are always interested in stupid reasoning and dumb arguments.

"What you mean, what *you* been through?"

So, I weaved him a tall tale about me and Albert having been born to parents who beat us and made us work all day in the hot sun and taught us to steal from neighbors and kept us locked up in the shed at nights and how we finally escaped only to be picked up by the law and put in an orphanage where the

93

treatment was even worse than what we had living at home until we couldn't take it no more and went on the run. How we stole crab apples and pies to eat and Mexican bandits had captured us and forced us to work in salt mines, and for sport, would force us to dance around a hat by shooting at our feet, until we snuck away from there and were dog ready to give up the ghost when the three of them stepped out onto the road.

"No, mister," I said. "Death would be a blessing. You'd be doing the Lord's work was you to rid the earth of Albert and me."

Albert tossed me the stink eye for I think he was worried I'd talk these miscreants into filling us both full of lead and ending our time on earth. To tell the truth, I was a little worried as well because I made the whole thing seem so believable that if I'd been telling the story to myself, Albert and me would already be dead, shot down like dogs. Seems like whenever I tell the truth, it sounds like I'm lying and whenever I lie, it seems like I'm telling the truth.

A single tear rolled down my cheek from my left eye, the only one I was ever able to get to do that whenever I'd be wanting pull at Sister Mary Virgin's heartstrings back at the orphanage to get out of going to early Mass on those cold mornings.

"Waugh!" Stumpy yelped. "Don't go to turning girlish on me. You ain't the only child in this here world ever had it rough, ain't that right, boys?"

The other two nodded.

"Besides," he said, "I've a moral code I go by. I don't shoot dogs, women, or children, though you two is just barely children, so you're just gonna have to face life's trials until somebody else puts you under. Like you yourself said, I don't think either of you is worth the price of bullets. Have you priced them lately?"

We shook our heads.

"Why would we?" Albert said. "We got no guns to put bullets in."

"Just as well, they practically cost a dang fortune," he said. "Getting so we might have to take up slingshots and use rocks instead. No, sir! Not hardly worth killing you two."

We watched them ride off with our stolen horses—now their stolen horses—and I could only hope they'd be caught as horse thieves and hanged, or be forced by Calamity Jane into fornicating, either of which would serve them right.

After they were good and gone out of sight, Albert looked more defeated than ever.

"The way our luck is running," he said, "we're never ever going to catch One-eye Texas Jack and get Banker Pettymoney's lady back. Heck, Ivory, we just seem to be going from pillar to post."

"Well, like you said before, Albert, you believe that our destinies was writ even before we were born. And, if true, that means that all that's happened to us was destined to be. And I reckon it ain't so much as setbacks as lessons to be learned. And I further reckon that if it's destined we catch One-eye Texas Jack and get back Mrs. Pettymoney, then all these troubles so far is just to test our mettle and sooner or later our misfortune will come to an end and we will prevail."

Now it was Albert's turn to look less sure of his own beliefs, but when one of us is down, the other must be up, like it was when we run down Rufus Buck and his gang. Of course, we had Gus to help for a time and, later, Preacher.

I wasn't at all sure whatever I said made any sense even to me, but I was doing my best to pick up Albert's spirits, just like he would mine if I was feeling lower than a snake's belly.

We started walking again and walked all day and well toward evening when, at once, a rumble and clatter came up behind us on an uphill grade, which had almost worn out our legs.

And there straining in their traces was a four-horse team pulling the Deadwood to Cheyenne stage under the cracking whip of a cuss with the brim of his hat pinned back to the crown, and next to him a feller holding a shotgun with one hand and holding onto the seat rail with the other.

Me and Albert ran out into the road waving our arms and jumping up and down while shouting for all we was worth.

The driver yelled for us to get the "hell" out of the way, and the man sitting next to him aimed his shotgun at us.

I told Albert to lay down in the road.

"Are you crazy, Ivory, that rig will run right over me and I'll be just as dead as if old age has killed me."

"Do what I said," I told him and flopped right down and so did he.

My ploy worked. I heard the driver yelling for the team to halt on top of which he called the horses some choice names, which I'm pretty sure they didn't understand the meanings of or they might have ignored him altogether.

I heard the driver say to the man with the shotgun, "Put it away, Bud, them two birds ain't holdup men, hell, they're barely men at all, just some wayward children what probably jumped off an orphan train."

The stage ground to a halt.

Me and Albert stood up slowly, our hands in the air.

"What you two peckerwoods doing laying down in the road like that?" the moustached driver said from atop the box. The one with the shotgun was also heavily moustached. They might have been brothers. The driver leaned off to the side and spat a stream and Shotgun did likewise, then each swiped his mouth with the gauntlet of his glove.

"We were robbed, our horses stole," I said.

"That right?" said Shotgun.

"It is right," said Albert.

"Well, who was it robbed you?"

"Couldn't say, but there was three of 'em."

"Three?" said the driver.

"One limped, the other two was just ugly," Albert said.

"That's most likely Deadwood Dick and his idiot brothers, Uriah and Fosdick," said Shotgun.

"Bud, here, blasted at 'em last time they tried to rob us, but the hosses jumped and threw off his aim, or them boys would be sleeping in a dirt bed as we speak," said the driver.

"Could we hitch a ride with you?" I asked.

"Sure, if you don't mind riding up top and got twelve dollars fare money each," the driver said.

I took out the leather pouch from under my shirt and spilled out the money into my hand. I already knew we were a dollar short.

"We're a dollar short," I said holding up the money.

"Bummers," said Shotgun to the driver. "Let 'em walk to Cheyenne. Maybe when they get there they'll have some gumption and get a job. Kids these days."

"Well, I reckon these boys has been through enough hell that a dollar more or less can't hurt. Climb up here, you ragamuffins."

So, we scampered up top and I handed the driver the money and he pocketed it right prompt.

"You fall off this stage while it's running, I won't stop and wait for you," he warned. "It's awful lonesome country, full of bandits and redskins."

We weren't sure why they made us ride up top, unless they didn't allow urchins inside. But it made no never mind to me as long as we weren't walking.

We grabbed the side rails and the driver urged and berated the team into the slow pull up the rest of the grade; then at the top, he cracked the whip and we went down the other side rocking and swaying to and fro. I shut my eyes for fear of seeing death in the form of being pitched off and under the team's hooves or the coach's wheels.

The driver and Shotgun "yee-hawed" as we went roaring down the grade toward who knew where or what. Those two in the box seemed pure maniacal with every mile and I didn't know how in the world they saw the road in the ever-growing darkness of dusk. I guessed maybe those horses could see it well enough—unless of course they were blind.

Finally, after being bounced in the air and gripping the rails so tight my hand and arm was nearly numb, the coach slowed, then turned in off the road and stopped at a lighted house.

"Change of hosses, folks," the driver called. "Time enough to relieve yourselves and grab a cup of coffee and a sandwich. Twenty minutes is all before we board again."

Me and Albert climbed down and walked off into the darkness and relieved our bladders, then came back and went inside the house, but we couldn't afford the sandwiches the woman inside was selling for two bits apiece—liverwurst and onion. Just the scent made my stomach growl. We was offered free coffee and took that gratefully and wished we'd at least had some bread to dunk in it.

We took our coffee outside and watched the men change out the team while the rest of the passengers were inside affording what we could not. The team changers cussed and spit the whole while, telling about them two orphans they'd picked up on the road what had been robbed by Deadwood Dick and his idiot brothers to a lot of guffaws.

Then, before we knew it, we were back on the road riding through the dark and I thought it was just as well we couldn't see the looming dangers as we held on for fear of instant demise with that coach rocking side to side as the driver made the turns, both of us so tired and worn out, it's a wonder we didn't fall asleep and roll off the top to our doom.

But suddenly the driver hauled back on the reins and sent the coach skittering sideways.

"What the hell!" he yelped.

"What's that alight in the road?" Shotgun growled under his moustaches.

"Fire."

"I can see it's a fire, but what's burning and why's it in the road?"

"Climb on down and take a gander."

We watched Shotgun climb down, but before he could reach back up for his blaster, a gravelly and familiar voice said, "Congratulations, you boobs, you've fallen for the dumbest ruse in the stagecoach-robbing business."

"Well, I'll be damned," the driver said, still holding Shotgun's shotgun.

"You will be damned if you go to try using that thing, dad," another voice said. "Hand'er down, stock first."

The driver did as he was told, as none other than the familiar face of the stumpy Deadwood Dick stepped forward out of the burning light holding a lantern up before him that caused his face to seem eerie and frightful, kinda like a jack-o'-lantern.

"You pilgrims climb out of that coach," he said. "You're being held up by none other than the notorious Deadwood Dick gang. Anyone tries being heroic will meet their doom."

I thought Dick was being overly dramatic with his tough talk, like a stage actor, for he sounded like one of the characters in Mr. DeWitt's novels. But those inside complied and stepped out: two ladies—one pretty, and one holding a small child who was less pretty—and two men dressed in suits who looked like dudes. The child was being whiny and complaining and the woman was doing her best to quiet the fussy infant.

"Hush, Harold," the lady holding him said. But it only made

the imp cry louder.

I tapped Albert on the leg and nodded toward a small trunk tied up top with us, and he knew what to do and was already loosening the cords as one of Dick's crew down below was troubling the pretty woman who wasn't holding the complaining child, speaking to her with lewd suggestions of what he'd like to do with her, while Deadwood himself was asking the driver to throw down the strongbox. But the driver said he couldn't, that it was bolted to the floor and the only one with a key was the stationmaster in Cheyenne.

"Modern times," said the driver, referring to the strongbox being bolted instead of just setting there loose like they once had been until all the robberies had forced the stage lines to come up with a better system. I learned all this later for it was not in any of my dime novels, but made thorough sense when I learned of it.

"You either toss it down or suffer the consequences," Deadwood Dick ordered. I was impressed that a road agent would have such a fine vocabulary.

Albert tapped my leg with his foot indicating he'd untied the cords holding the trunk, and together we leaned over the top and dropped it straight down on the one holding the confiscated shotgun—that gimpy fellow from earlier—as he stood on the far side of the coach away from the other two and the passengers. There was just a thunk! He didn't make a sound as that trunk knocked him cold.

Albert and me scrambled down that side and I got the shotgun and Albert jerked the pistol out of the man's holster.

"What was that noise?" Dick called to the coldcocked companion from the other side of the coach.

No answer.

"Fosdick, you okay over there?"

I heard the pretty woman on the other side saying: "Unhand

me, you brute!"

In the chaos, I handed the shotgun up to the driver and he cut loose with both barrels that left no mistake as to their power.

"BOOM!"

Albert came 'round the back of the coach, the miscreant's cocked revolver in his hand, shouting: "There is little worse than a molester of innocent women."

I was quite proud of Albert. He showed real grit, even if the man he'd warned was lying sprawled out and terribly dead, the front of him ripped and ragged and bleeding from a dozen or more wounds. Ditto: Deadwood Dick. Both defunct.

Everybody was nervously jubilant as Albert and me and the shotgun messenger tied the still-addled remaining outlaw over the saddle of the same horse we'd stolen from Barney in Deadwood and then had stolen from us. Real irony, and I don't reckon at the current rate, Barney was ever going to see his horse again.

"You boys is likely to get some sort of reward from the stage line for your heroic act," the driver said.

Well that sounded pretty good.

"In the meanwhile, here's your fare money back as a show of my personal appreciation. It's always a good day when I can plant miscreants in Dakota soil. You boys ride the best of the horses and tie the other'n with that halfwit over its back behind the boot, would you?"

How could we possibly refuse?

CHAPTER 6

So we followed that stage all along the way, stopping every so often for changes of horse teams at places such as Chugwater Station and Six Mile Ranch and Hat Creek and the like, with tales of the attempted robbery repeated and expanding at every stop as told by the driver, Mayfly Morse, and his messenger, Bud Dilly (later killed). Our prisoner put up such a fuss carping and complaining about being slung across the back of the horse, our ears hurt. We finally untied him and let him sit upright with fair warning that if he so much as tried to run, we'd blow out his intentions. He said we'd have no trouble with him and that he looked forward to a soft cot and three squares a day in the jail.

"A word of advice," he said. "Don't ever go into the outlaw life, it just don't pay. Take it from me. Boys, my trifling days of wrongdoing are over. I intend on taking up reading the good book while serving my time in the calaboose, no matter how long that might take. I am truly grateful you dropped that trunk on my head before I did something worse than what all I done." Then he offered to shake our hands as we turned him over to the sheriff in Lusk.

And thus it was, we finally made Cheyenne and the driver had been right. Albert and me were given one hundred dollars reward money for foiling the stage robbery and capturing one of the bandits, with the other two less fortunate. We were also put up in our own separate rooms at the Inter-Ocean Hotel, a three-story square building that looked big enough to hold all the folks of Last Whisky at the same time and still have room left over.

"And eats are on the stage company too," we were told by the stage-line manager. "Got a real fine saloon and restaurant right on the first floor. Just charge everything to the company. I'll see your horses are put up and cared for at the stable for whenever you get ready to leave. You boys enjoy."

"Well, for a pair of ragamuffins like us," I said to Albert standing there in the big lobby, "we sure didn't make out too bad, now, did we?"

Albert was gazing up at the crystal chandelier hanging over our heads.

"I never thought I'd find myself in such a swell place as this," he said.

"And me even less so," I said. "And it ain't costing us a dime."

For a time, we just stood there grinning at each other.

We were given the keys to our rooms, 212 and 214, right next to each other. Albert stood studying the room numbers and said, "Ivory, it don't make sense. Shouldn't it be . . ." Then I pointed out to him that room 213 was directly across the hall.

"That's how I reckon they do it in the big city," I said, "back and forth, not all in a row. They're sophisticated."

"Oh."

"Let's say we get cleaned up, then go and find the sheriff or something, see can we learn more about locating this here Robbers Roost. I'm sure he must have heard of it."

Albert nodded.

"Maybe it wouldn't hurt to eat something first," he said. "That stage-line grub ain't so good."

We agreed to meet in half an hour, then nearly soon as I got into my room Albert came knocking at my door.

"Ivory, there is a bathtub in my room and all you have to do to draw water is turn the handle and it comes right on up."

"We better make it an hour then," I said. "For I've got a week's worth of dirt to scrub off."

Well, when the time was up and the hot water turned cool, I sure hated to climb out of that bath. I never felt so clean in my life, and feeling clean can give a body a whole new outlook on life.

I waited for Albert down in the hotel lobby and wondered what was keeping him, then finally he showed up looking sheepish.

"Well, what's with you and how come you were up there so long?" I asked.

"Ivory, you ain't gonna believe what happened."

"What? You find a fish in that bathtub?"

"No. You remember that woman on the stage, the pretty one that that outlaw tried molesting before we sprung into action?" *Sprung into action? Sounded like Albert had been reading as many of the dime novels as myself. I'd have to remember that line.*

"Well, sure I do," I said. "What about her?"

She showed up at my door knocking away and I had to climb out soaking wet and wrap a towel around me, 'cause I thought it was you, and, well, it wasn't. It was her."

"What'd she want?"

"Said she'd be honored to take me—and well, maybe you, I reckon she meant us, though she didn't say you—but I think she meant the two of us, out to dinner this evening. Said she was mighty grateful we stopped something worse happening to her and wanted to show her gratitude. I swear, the good luck just keeps on coming, don't it?"

"Sounds like maybe she's smitten with you—like the women are in the dime novels when a hero saves them."

"Do you think it possible?"

"Sure, why not?"

"Goldang!"

"Did you get her name?"

"Well, of course I did, Ivory. I ain't no durn fool. It's Geneva Pearlfeather. Said she's visiting her uncle here in Cheyenne."

"From what I seen of her, the name seems to fit. She's gem pretty and delicate too."

This seemed to please Albert even more than he was already pleased.

"Just don't act like no schoolboy around her when she takes you out to dinner. How old would you say she is, anyway?"

He pondered it for a thoroughly enjoyable moment.

"I reckon maybe five, six years older'n me, not that much. You think that's too much older for me, Ivory?"

"Don't see why it should be. Heck, half these men out here in the west marry women ten, twenty years younger, I don't see why this Geneva being a few years older'n you should matter. Obviously, it doesn't matter to her."

He looked as happy as a kid eating ice cream on Christmas morning.

"You know," I said. "We might be washed up, but these duds of ours sure ain't. They're stiff with dust and sweat and if I wear them ten more minutes I'm going to have to take me another bath. Let's see can we find a place to buy some new ones, shirt and pants, at least. That way, you'll look proper when Miss Pearlfeather takes you out to eat."

"I was thinking the same thing, Ivory, I almost didn't get dressed for not wanting to get dirty again."

So we asked the fellow at the front desk where we could buy some new threads. He was a young feller with thick blondish hair and pitted cheeks and he drew a map for us, telling us to take a right out the front door and follow from there. We thanked him and headed out.

The place was called CLOTHING AND GENTS FUR-

NISHING GOODS and it was located on the corners of Eddy and 16th streets. Real fancy looking it was too and as soon as we stepped in, there was an old gentleman finely dressed who looked upon us like we were something needed to be set out in the alley.

"How may I assist you?" he said dryly.

"Why, this is a clothing store, ain't it?" Albert piped up.

"Yes, clearly it is," the feller said.

"Well, then," said Albert. "I reckon that's how you can help us."

The feller cleared his throat real loud, then said, "Perhaps you'd do better down at the Congregational Church basement where they collect items for the indigent."

Albert tossed me that look over the word "indigent."

"Means, poor, mostly," I said.

Albert reached into the pocket of those dirt-streaked and sweat-stiffed jeans and took the wad of his share of our stagecoach reward money.

"Mister, does this look like I'm indignant to you?"

"Indigent," I corrected.

"Whatever," Albert growled through clamped jaws. "Well, does it?"

The man shook his head and his attitude quickly changed when he saw Albert's money.

"Why, no, sir, I only thought that . . . Please, step over this way."

I followed as he took Albert and me over to a shelf of fancy pants and fancy shirts, kind of like those sateen ones we had before.

"No, thanks," Albert said and spied a shelf of plain denim jeans and common cotton shirts and told the man, "We'll have two shirts and two pairs of jeans and two pairs of socks each."

"Do you know your size?" the man offered.

Albert looked down at himself, then said, "This here is my size, and that yonder is my friend, Ivory, and that is his size."

That feller must have had a keen eye for sizes for he picked out a shirt and a pair of jeans for Albert and me and told us to go into this little room and try them on and we did and they fit perfect and when Albert saw this he said, "*Gol-dog,* you believe it?"

"Let's just leave our old things here in this waste can," I said, and that's what we did. We come out wearing our new shirts and pants and handed him over the extras for him to wrap up, which he did and tied with string so we could carry them easily and we paid him, feeling like newborn children whilst looking at ourselves in a tall mirror.

"Now, we just need new hats and boots," I said. And so, we picked some out and hats as well. And we came out of that store looking like real desperados but for one thing, guns. We needed some new guns to replace the ones we left when attacked by Indians.

Since we were a good distance from the hotel, we decided to forego eating there and instead went into a place called Ramsey's Restaurant after we stopped at the telegraph office so I could send Banker Pettymoney a wire as to our current location. Then we went and followed our noses toward the rest of the way toward the smell of food cooking that drew us in as surely as if Mr. Ramsey himself was standing outside and dragged us in by the arm.

It was just a common eatery, nothing at all fancy about it, but it sure had a lot of people eating there.

Albert and me took a table by the window and stared up at the chalkboard what had the morning menu written in chalk on it.

"What you going to have, Ivory?" Albert asked.

"Everything," I said.

He grinned.

"Me too."

A pretty little Negro waitress the color of coffee with cream stirred in caught my attention, because she was not only cute as a puppy, but she was one of the few colored gals I'd see around that wasn't sweating over a steaming tub of laundry or carting steamer trunks on their backs.

"How do?" she said as she walked up to our table and gave a slight curtsy but her gaze was straight on me. "You gentlemens like coffee?"

"Like something to eat." I said.

"Why, of course, got so many folks in this morning I forgot what all I was doing." Again, talking straight at me. I glanced at Albert and he had a sheepish grin like a pal will do when he knows what is up.

So, we ordered our meal of sausages and fried eggs and biscuits with butter and honey, and grits, and coffee, of course.

"I'll go fetch it," she said, again with the curtsy.

"Don't you need to write it down?" I said.

"No sweetness, Jazzy's got a good memory."

"So, your name's Jazzy?" I said, doing my best to keep her at the table.

"How'd you guess," she laughed, causing me to feel like a fool until she asked me what my name was and I told her and she repeated it nice and soft, "Ivory"; then she turned and walked off toward the kitchen and I studied on how she walked too, how her hips and bottom shifted to and fro like a well-put-together machine. Albert told me to put my eyes back in my head.

"You know something," Albert said, "I'd say we're doing all right here in Cheyenne, you and me, wouldn't you?"

"Don't know yet, but it's starting to look that way."

Jazzy returned soon with a coffeepot and two cups and set

them down and poured them full and gifted me one more big ol' smile and I gave her one of mine, back—showing all my teeth, for the good Lord blessed me with real good teeth.

When she brought our food on china plates, it seemed she'd wanted to linger but other diners were calling her to their table to refill their cups or bring them something more, like a slice of pie or whatever. Albert and me shoveled in our food like they're not making any more of it—ever.

Pretty soon Jazzy returned with the coffeepot and started to refill our cups.

Albert waved a hand over his cup saying he was about to burst, but I quickly said, "Oh, yes, ma'am, pretty please," as I looked up into her golden brown eyes while she leaned over and filled my cup nice and slow, like she was enjoying the linger as much as me. But like everything, comes a time when it has to end and it did when the level of Arbuckle reached the rim of my cup.

"Will that be all for you, Mister Ivory?"

"Maybe a slice of pie if you got any."

"Well, what kinds do you like?"

"What kinds do you have?"

So she named them and when she finished I said, "What was that first one again?"

"Rhubarb. That's my favorite."

"Well, now ain't that something," I said. "That's my favorite too."

She smiled all the more and I smiled all the more too, and even Albert was smiling. Once she sashayed off, I just couldn't keep from watching and she seemed to guess I was because she took her time in the sashaying.

"I'm considering maybe moving here to Cheyenne after we take care of that evil killer and kidnapper," I said, suddenly feeling like maybe Last Whisky didn't seem so attractive a place to call home anymore now that I seen a big town.

"You know," Albert said, "I was kinda thinking the same thing."

I knew he was already smitten by this Geneva Pearlfeather woman from the stage, but I didn't think he was that far gone already.

"Maybe we should concentrate first at the job at hand," I said.

"You're right. No sense dreaming of being rich men when our pockets are still empty," Albert said.

"I'm still against joining up with this Pinkerton fellow Petty-money sent for if and when he makes his way here."

"I know you are, Ivory. But doesn't it seem to figure that if we had a professional like a Pink on our side we might catch One-eye Texas Jack sooner and get on back here and maybe settle down?"

"What about your ma, Albert? Wouldn't she be disappointed you not returning to Last Whisky?"

"Oh, I figured she'd like it well enough here when I sent for her."

"Still, what do we do about this Pink if he shows up?" I said.

"Nothing," Albert said.

I was about to protest but then Jazzy came back and set a slice of pie down in front of me large enough to use as a doorstop and leaned in real close with one hand on my back for support. Whatever she was wearing smelled like all the flowers in all the world was blooming on her skin, that perfume the rich ladies get from France.

"Sliced you an extra-sized piece," Jazzy said. "Strong young man such as yourself needs to keep up his strength."

"Oh, yes, ma'am," I said. "I'm feeling mighty puny here lately, that extra pie will help a whole lot to make me feel real manly again, you know what I mean."

It was all I could do to restrain myself from kissing her with her mouth and soft lips just inches from my face.

"Ain't seen you boys in here before," she said, finally straightening up again. "You all just move to town, or passing through?"

I glanced across the table at Albert and he was just sitting there about to bust, big ol' smile on him like he can't hold it in what he's thinking.

"We're bounty hunting a terrible killer," I said. "Albert here and me. And as soon as we catch him, I reckon we're thinking about returning to this nice little town. Seems real pleasant, like a good place for a man to settle down. Would you say that was so, Jazzy?"

"Oh, it's a right proper place," she said. "Real friendly folks. Is you the real friendly type, Ivory?"

"Why even the devil hisself loves me," I said with a wink.

Then a man's voice called from the back where the kitchen was, telling her to "Hustle up. Customers waiting, Jazzy!"

"I got to get on," she said. "Maybe I'll see you in here later if you hungry for supper."

"Ivory is always, hungry, Miss," Albert said. And I nodded in agreement like a donkey drinking from a trough, then we parted. I cast one last lingering look. My heart felt about to burst with anticipation, of what, I couldn't even explain.

Albert watched me murder that piece of pie by forking it into my yap while I kept trying to track Jazzy with my eyeballs.

When I finished, and all but licked the plate while hoping Jazzy would find time to come back around—which she didn't because the place was by then full and she was running around from table to table, though occasionally tossing me looks—I finally set my fork aside, and Albert and me made our exit.

"I don't reckon I ever et so much in my life," Albert said, and then gave a loud burp that set him to grinning foolishly. So I burped too and we both laughed.

"I reckon we need to go and find the sheriff or whatever it is they got for law in this town," I said. "See can't we get a line on this Robbers Roost."

"We should get something to shoot, unless you just planning on flinging rocks at One-eye Texas Jack when we catch up with him," Albert said.

"You're reading my mind," I said.

"Really, Ivory?" He seemed smug that I would have said so.

So, we made some inquires and learned where there was a gunsmith not far, over on 17th Street, and figured that now that we have a little money why not just buy holsters to carry the guns in that we purchase. Once there, Albert bought a bird's head Colt, like what Billy had, and it's a Schofield Russian Model for me on account of the size of it; figure I run out of bullets I can clobber somebody with it, or hammer a nail, I need to build a house.

When we finished with everything we got directions to the jail. Bigger than I thought, and went in.

A man in a blue serge jacket with a metal badge pinned to the lapel and gray trousers was concentrating on hanging a photograph on the wall whilst standing on a rickety looking chair, a nail protruding from his mouth and a hammer in one hand and the framed picture leaning against the wall there on the floor.

He turned his head when we entered.

"What's it I can do for you, boys?" he mumbled around the nail,

"We're here to report a crime—a kidnapping of a woman," I said.

He removed the nail from his mouth and said, "Your wife?" Then he laughed so hard he near fell off the chair.

"We can wait until you're finished," I said.

He turned back to the job at hand, pounded the nail in, squatted down for the photograph and placed it on the nail, then fixed it just so.

"That look straight to you?" he said either to me or Albert or maybe both.

We agreed that it did and he climbed down and sat behind a wide wood desk, the top of which was covered by a blotter and a silver pen set with an ink bottle, and a wire basket of papers. The chair squeaked on springs that allowed it to be tipped back and forth when he sat in it. He was a man of considerable bulk.

"Now, what's this about a kidnapping?"

So, we explained it all and he listened even as he packed a pipe with tobacco from a canister, tamped it down, then struck a match and puffed on it until he exhaled a bloom of smoke. The sucking noise was a bit irritating.

"So, you can see, Sheriff," I started to say when he raised a fat palm and stopped me.

"I ain't the sheriff, I'm just one of the deputies who is watching the jail today. Sheriff's way out in the county somewhere." Then he did a funny thing and winked and added: "Might be visiting the Widow Blaine, if you know what I mean."

We didn't, but sort of figured it out if, indeed, the sheriff, whoever he was, had been out visiting the Widow Blaine, whoever she was.

We asked him for the law's help in capturing One-eye Texas Jack Crowfoot for the crimes of bank robbery and kidnapping.

"You say this happened in Deadwood?"

We told him no, that it was before Deadwood up in Booker Creek in the Montana Territory. We both wondered how he could have forgotten when we'd just pretty much finished telling him the story. Maybe he got lost when we mentioned the Indian attack on our camp.

"Wasn't you paying attention?" Albert said as sternly as a

body his age could say to a fully grown man and officer of the law. The big man eyed him through the cloud of his pipe smoke but held his water.

"Well, wherever it happened," he said, "that's not here, wouldn't you agree?"

"Yes, sir, we know that," I said.

"Well, then you'd further know, I've got no jurisdiction if it wasn't around here. 'Scuse me while I go out back and water my posies."

We watched as he stood and headed down a hallway.

"He's just being obtuse," I said.

Albert punched me on the shoulder and said, "Dang it, Ivory, how many times have I told you?"

"Means slow-witted, mostly. But whether or not he's doing it on purpose, I can't say."

In a few minutes, he returned and I noticed a small wet spot there on his trousers' front but did my best to ignore it.

"So, we can expect no help then?" I said as he eased himself back down into the chair.

"Sorry, not from me. Now you could wait for the sheriff to return and ask him, he might could help you out—though, I doubt it."

"When will he be back?" Albert said.

The deputy shrugged, picked up his pipe from the desk, and relit it again, his pale, red-veined cheeks working like a bellows.

"Impossible to say," he said, snapping out the match, then using the other end as a toothpick to dig away at his teeth. "Could be back tomorrow, or a month from now. He's got the whole county to cover and I heard there may have been some killings up around Johnson County, so who knows. That, and how long he visits the Widow Blaine."

Albert and I looked at each other.

"Well, is it at least possible to tell us if you've ever heard of the Robbers Roost?" I said.

He arched one eyebrow.

"Heard of it. You reckon that's where your man has gotten off to?"

"So we believe," Albert said.

"Sorry, sonny, can't help you."

"Well, that's a hell of a note, mister!" Albert exclaimed. He was fuming mad and I didn't blame him, but he had to be careful about riling up a lawman and I was on edge the deputy might just jump over the desk and slap snot out of Albert and I was getting ready to pistol-whip him if he tried, but likely as not that big fool would have slapped snot out of both of us.

But instead, the lawman scratched something with his pen on a piece of paper and held it out and Albert took it.

"What's this?"

"The names of some fellers who might assist you in your plight. Now, move along, it's time for my dinner."

With this, he stood and took his hat from a hook and settled it onto his head and grabbed a ring of keys and just about pushed us out the door, then locked it behind us.

Albert just had to get one more dig in at the man by saying: "I don't see why you're locking the door, don't know of anybody who would want to break into a dang jail."

"I told you to get along or you'll be my first customers of the day," the deputy said roughly back, and I don't reckon he was being obtuse about it, either.

We walked a little ways down the street, then stopped, and Albert showed me what was written on the paper; in a surprisingly nice cursive were the words: *Pallor Bros. Chink Town.*

"Say, isn't that the same name Billy talked about might could give us information?" I said.

"You're right," Albert said. "But what is this Chink Town mean?"

"Chink is a slanderous name for Chinese fellows, where they live at," I said. "But I got no clue as to where it is."

"Who we gonna ask?"

Just about then I spotted an interesting name of a place across the street.

"Come'n," I said, tugging Albert's coat sleeve.

"Turn loose of me, fool, I can walk on my own!" Albert yelped.

"Yes, but you're likely to get run over by one of these drunken teamster drivers roaring up and down the street; I'm just trying to watch out for you 'count of if you get killed, I'd have to find ol' One-eye by my lonesome."

We waited to try and make it safely across without certain death from the traffic.

I pointed to the sign over the door of our destination.

Cheyenne Rooster Club

"Bound to be someone inside knows where this Chink Town is," I said.

But just as we were about to cross over trying once more not to get squashed by some mad cussing teamster, we were hailed by our names being called out.

"Oh, Albert, Ivory!"

We stopped and looked around and coming up the sidewalk was none other than Geneva Pearlfeather and a lanky cuss dressed in a pigeon gray suit and wearing a sugarloaf hat of matching color.

"Oh," Geneva started by saying. "I'm so glad I caught up with you, Albert," pretty much ignoring me altogether. "This is my uncle, Buster Brick, and I was telling him all about you, how you saved us all from being robbed and molested by the stage robbers. He'd very much enjoy taking us to the matinee at the opera house and later this evening dinner. Would that be all right with you, Albert?"

Albert stood tongue-tied, mostly, gawping and staring and almost drooling at the sight of the older pretty woman.

"I reckon," he finally blurted.

"Gee, that's swell," she said, and looked him over, then added: "Uncle is taking me shopping for a new dress and shoes. Perhaps we should take you along and buy you something proper to wear to the opera. Would you find fault with my suggestion, *Albert*?" Said it all gushy and sweet.

"No, I reckon not," he said, looking down at himself. "But what I got on is just been bought."

"Oh, I know," she said, "and your outfit looks terrific—for a cowboy. But the opera is so special . . ." She let that comment hang out there like a pear waiting to be plucked and Albert did just that, he plucked it.

"Fine," he said. "You're right."

"Oh, good!" she exclaimed and threw her arms around him and gave him a big hug. I thought maybe I was going to have to prop him up when she let loose of him. The big galoot with her stuck out a paw that looked like it hadn't seen a lick of work, ever. Albert shook it first, then mister fancy pants offered it to me.

"And you're Ivory," he said. "Pleased to meetcha."

So, I shook it too. I've shook washerwoman's hands that were rougher.

"And after we're done with the shopping, we'll drop Albert back at the hotel, Ivory, so not to worry," Geneva said.

"I ain't worried. Albert can take care of himself," I said so as not to hamstring him by showing my concern.

"Good," she clapped, then poked one arm through Uncle Brick's and one through my pal Albert's and started up the street. Albert threw me a "what the heck" look, and off they traipsed down the sidewalk.

To tell the truth, though, I was a bit worried about Albert. I didn't know those people and they seemed too slick by a mile to suit me. But both me and Albert was of that age now where we maybe weren't full-grown men, but we were no longer boys, either.

CHAPTER 7

I turned my attention to the Rooster Club and skedaddled across the street, and once within, there was plenty of loud noise like you might have at a hanging, but I reckoned it was on account of it being Saturday and nobody had much to do but drink and have a bunch of fun.

An entire big room of folks moved about under a cloud of cigar smoke like ghosts, the smoke so thick you couldn't hardly make out nothing. Somebody was hammering on a piano and some others were singing raucously. Singing might have been too strong a word for it—more like cats getting their tails caught under rocking chairs.

The place seemed to me the center of gaiety and action and I sure could use some of that, what with me feeling bereft as I was over Albert having a gal and gone off with her and leaving me on my own hook. Geneva was not only pretty, but, being older as well, made her a lot more tempting for a feller me and Albert's age. I reckon it was every young man's dream to be loved on by a woman that was pretty and older, one that could teach him the ways of the world, so to speak. I confess to having a certain attraction to older women myself ever since my friendship with Sister Mary Virgin. I used to lay abed at nights and fantasize about the two of us running off someplace where we could sit by the ocean and read books and she could teach me all she knew from her extensive knowledge of literature, philosophy, and other thoughtful pursuits. Then she would toss off her religious robes and beliefs out of love for me and turn me into a bona fide man.

But, of course, I knew that was never going to happen, not in a million years—even though she did run off with a man, it wasn't me. Still, a fella can dream, can't he, for what good are dreams if you can't dream them?

Being inside the Rooster Club, I did not see but one rooster, and that the one painted over the door, big and red and wearing cowboy spurs and a canted high-crown hat with curled brim and one eye cocked to those of us down below with a knowing wink as if it shared a secret. Sort of like: "All who enter here is in for a really good time, you can bet your boots."

I could hear the high-pitched laughter of females stirring the smoky air. Most generally women weren't allowed unescorted into saloons—least the saloons I knew of. But it seemed from the sounds that there must have been a goodly number of women in the Rooster to entertain the galoots. Their perfume mixed with the scent of cigar smoke and sweat and maybe some other human smells as well, sort of left me feeling feverish, over what I couldn't rightly say, but I reasoned a beer might help.

I worked my way up to the bar, and being tall as I am and looking the part of a regular buckaroo, nobody paid me notice.

First thing that caught my attention whilst I was waiting to get served by one of the four barkeeps—all of them fat with oily hair parted down the middle and wearing garters on their sleeves and aprons—was a large painting overhead of two nearly naked women frolicking in a stream, wearing little more than smiles and flimsy scarves you could see through. They were big haunchy gals that must have not minded the painter painting them that way. I reckon it must have been sort of thrilling to feel so free as prancing about nearly naked in front of some painter feller that way. I thought almost immediately of Billy bathing buck-naked in the creek. I guess there is just some folks don't care for the restrictions of clothes. I'd never seen such art, at least not in the art books Sister Mary Virgin shared with me, which was mostly paintings of churches with saints and quaint houses and the Lord nailed to the cross with blood running down his side.

I was still staring up at the painting when a voice shouted over the din and hubbub, "What'll it be, boyo?"

"I'll have a iced beer, as advertised." I pointed to the chalkboard on the wall.

He looked me over and then pulled the long handle with a beer glass underneath and swiped off the foamy head and said: "Ten cents, bub." So, I slapped a silver dollar atop the wood just like I owned the place and was the richest fool in all of Cheyenne. He must have liked the sound it made for he smiled, showing real nice white teeth, at least the three or four yet remaining in his mouth, and brought me back change, then hurried off to help those others lined up like cattle at a watering hole. In some places they were standing two and three deep, many of them with women clinging to them mewing and remonstrating at them—the sort of women like what was in that painting, only not so haunchy and healthy looking. Most of the real ones were fairly skinny and a bit homely with unhealthy looking skin. The cowboys they hung on to didn't seem to mind.

I did notice as I was sipping that cold beer—a real treat from most places that served it warm—that most of the ladies had the same white silvery hair done in curls or waves, and their cheeks were rouged and lips painted blood red. But what really caught my attention was how low-cut their dresses were in front, the bigger ones, so that their bosoms looked like baby bottoms sticking out.

A fellow in a cream-colored western hat next to me at the bar said, "This is some lonesome existence, ain't it?"

I turned to look at him and he stood under a cream-colored

Boss of the Plains hat and was short and round and wearing a real nice buckskin jacket with fringed sleeves and beaded front, and his pants were buckskin too. I glanced down at his footwear: fancy beaded moccasins. If he hadn't been so white, I'd a thought him an Indian. Head to toe he was a specimen with the white silk shirt under his jacket and the vermillion sash around his middle bulk, which held the butts of pearl-handled Navies.

"What do you mean, lonesome?" I asked. "Seems to me one of the liveliest places I've ever seen."

His hangdog eyes fell on me like I was the most ill-informed creature he ever saw.

"Oh, it's lively all right," he said, holding his beer glass in one hand and resting the other on one of the Navies. "But that's the whole thing about lonesomeness. Don't matter how many folks is around you, you can still be made to feel awfully alone. Take those Cyprians yonder draped on them galoots begging 'em for a drink and offering in exchange a roll in the hay. They're all just plain lonesome. I've known my share of barroom tarts, and have yet to meet a one didn't put on an act, not only for you, but for herself, and everybody feels better for a little while. But it always returns, that loneliness and deep inside we're all terribly sad creatures. Lots of 'em poor creatures take their own lives after a time of so much lonesomeness; they just can't stand it no more and drink mercury or slit their wrists. Lots of 'em are dope fiends in order so they can sell the most precious thing God ever gave them to whatever yahoo's got the price."

Well, that sure took some of the starch out of me.

"Bill and me was rounders once," he continued without a single question from me. "There probably wasn't a good whore—nor a bad one—west of the big muddy we didn't . . ."

Suddenly the fellow's eyes got misty and wounded instead of just hangdog and he struggled to get the words out until he downed a shot of whiskey followed by a long swallow of his beer, then blew his nose on a pocket rag that looked like a miniature flag of the United States he'd taken from a pocket, then stuffed it back into its hidey-hole.

"Sorry, sonny," he said, and reached into the breast pocket of his shirt for a stogie and lighted it. "I get the maudlins whenever I think of my late pard. You might've heard of him—Wild Bill, Prince of the Pistoleers."

"Mister Hickok?"

"The one and only I know of. The original. He was but thirty-nine years old when he crossed the River Styx, and not willingly so, I venture to guess."

I immediately thought of the woman, Jane, who called herself Calamity and said she was Wild Bill's wife.

"Say," I said. "I met his wife a few days back along the trail."

"Oh?"

"Said her name was Calamity Jane."

He nearly spit up his beer.

"That old tart! She still running around claiming to be Bill's wife?"

"That's what she said. Is she not?"

He shook his head.

"Jane's a loon and alcoholic, but one thing she is not is Wild Bill's wife."

Then, as if remembering something, he patted the pocket of his jacket and reached inside and took out a folded piece of lavender stationery.

"This Bill gave me whilst we was up in Deadwood to send to his real bride, Agnes Lake. Said to me as if he had a premonition that the end of the trail was near for him: 'Charley, can I count on you to see Agnes gets this?' and I said 'sure, Bill, you know you can.' I thought he was just being maudlin again like he could sometimes get; his moods could swing like a hanged man in a Kansas wind. Then one week later he was dead, bleeding out on a dirty sawdust floor in Nuttall and Mann's Number Ten. I never cared for that place, personally, nor some of the friends he'd made there."

He paused and shook his head and took another good swallow of beer and brushed his eyes again. And without saying another word he began reading the note. And you'd a thought with all that surrounding noise I wouldn't have been able to hear what he was reading, but it came across as surely as if the two of us were sitting in a library somewhere.

"Agnes Darling, if such should be we never meet again, while firing my last shot, I will gently breathe the name of my wife— Agnes—and with wishes even for my enemies I will make the plunge and try to swim to the other shore." J.B. Hickok Wild Bill.

He sighed then and folded the piece of paper and placed it back into the envelope and then put it back into the inside pocket he'd taken it from and gently patted himself before draining his glass.

"No, old pard," he said, "all is lonesome since the passing of my friend. It seems impossible that a man of such vigor has been struck dead in the prime of his being, for such a man was he, none who knew him could imagine him cold and stiff lying forever in the ground. And if you think it mattered one bit that he always got first turn with gals and me second, and that galoots bought him drinks simply because of who he was and ignored me," he paused to swing his arm wide, "well, you'd be mistaken. I didn't mind one bit having to wait my turn, except just once."

Again, he heaved a sigh but did not this time get misty-eyed.

"Her name was Sing-Lee, or some such, which means Beautiful Bird, or some such. And she was that indeed, and I never knew what it was she saw in me after ol' Bill had topped her, but she later, when it was just her and I alone up in the room, she let it be known that Bill wasn't near the lover I was, and I can't tell you how that made my heart swell."

My beer was slowly getting warm, for I was fascinated by this tale of this strange little man who might have possibly been taller lying down than he was standing up.

I took a swallow of my beer and he took a swallow of his.

"I do think when I was with her," he continued, "I was for the first time joyous in spirit as I've never been before or since."

I noticed the silver band on his finger.

"You married?" I asked.

He glanced down as if he'd forgotten he had fingers.

"Why, yes," he said. "Going on almost twenty years."

"Well, doesn't your wife make you happy?"

He softly smiled as if I was not all there in the brains department.

"Wives is different," is all he said.

"I only have one great regret in my life," he said.

"That your wife found out about this Chinese woman?" I said stupidly.

"No, she didn't, and I'd never tell her. I have a word for men who confess to their wives their sins."

"What's that?" I asked.

"Cowards," he said.

"Oh."

"No, my one regret is that Bill had gotten first dibs with my great love that time, and broke the china, so to speak. That's one I can never forgive him for, and I hope the good Lord forgives me for saying that."

I didn't know what to reply. Seemed my whole life I just had that sort of face that made folks want to spill their beans. Even someone as refined and dedicated to her life as the Lord's bride, Sister Mary Virgin, had told me things I doubt she told anyone else, not even her fellow sisters. I guess I was just always a real good listener.

"I'm sure the Lord won't hold a thing like that against you," I told the little man. "I mean, I bet if he forgives killers and pickpockets and card cheats, he'd surely not hold such feelings against you."

The little man nodded in affirmation and stuck out his hand, also small, and soft as a child's.

"Name's Colorado Charley Utter," he said. "Glad to make your acquaintance."

"Likewise," I said and gave him my name and he said Ivory was a right fine handle.

He pumped my hand like he was trying to draw water from deep in the earth.

"Let me buy you a drink, old Pard," he said.

"Say, before you do, can I ask if you've ever heard of the Pallor brothers?"

He gave me a funny blanched look.

"Hell on wheels, them two. Bad news and bad business. I'd steer clear of the likes of them. Bill almost doused their lights once, right here in Cheyenne."

"How about a place called Robbers Roost?"

"Heard of it, don't know where it is," he said.

The barkeeps were all at the other end.

"I'll go rassle one of them pump pullers up," said Charley and disappeared in the crowd never to return.

Well, I stood there nursing my beer, now as warm as spit, and studied the mass of humanity swirling about, talking loud, laughing, arguing, cussing, and thought about what the funny little man told me about a lonesome existence. Pretty soon a fight broke out between two fellers and before you know it, they were rassling around on the floor trying to punch the head of the other one and bite off ears until of a sudden the loud crack

126

of a firearm went off.

You'd be surprised how something like that gets everyone's attention. It sure got mine and set my ears to ringing.

Wading into that whole bunch was a big red-headed man, hatless, and a napkin still stuck in the front of his shirt.

"You damn idjits want to fight, want to kill each other, well, I'll help you along," he said, then he pointed the revolver at the two as the rest of the crowd fell back. His cocking of the hammer, and the three small clicks it made, sounded to me like a skeleton's teeth eating crackers.

The pair on the floor broke apart like exhausted lovers and lay there panting and breathing hard, busted noses dripping blood and swollen eyes notwithstanding.

"Git on up!" the big man shouted. Then he looked toward the bar and said, "Lou, these fellas bust any furniture they owe you for?"

One of the bartenders said no.

Then the redhead waved the fighters on out of the doors and the crowd once more went back to what it had been doing— having a good time.

I was just about to go on back to the hotel room when a large gal with big bosoms swelling out of the top of her fancy red and black striped dress sidled up and latched herself onto me.

"Hey, Nig," she said. "How's about buying a gal a drink?"

She was as tall as I but weighed again twice as much. I never did have any bulk, all gristle and bone, Albert said about me. Course he was nobody to talk. I told him he was too light to fight and too thin to win, always good for a laugh whenever I said it.

"Well, I don't know," I said to the woman. "I was just getting ready to go."

But she was latched onto me more so than those two fighting

fellers had latched on to each other that the lawman just chased out.

"Come'n. Is it you don't like me?" she said in this peaked little voice that belied her size.

"Like you? I don't even know you."

My remark was indeed weak, as I hoped not to insult her. She was, after all, a woman, and I'd been taught while in the orphanage to be polite, especially to females.

"Remember, Ivory, we're the fairer sex," Sister Mary Virgin told me on one of our afternoon strolls around the grounds. "It is never right to hit a woman, under any circumstances."

"Yes, Sister."

"Well, all right then," I said to the big gal and waved one of the barkeeps over. The two of them exchanged winks.

"What'll it be, Roxy?" he said.

"Cocktail, Sam."

"And you, mister?"

"I'll have the same," I said, for my beer glass was empty and besides I never had a cocktail before and I was feeling emboldened, but I couldn't tell you why.

Sam right quick mixed us two cocktails.

"Two dollars," he said, setting them down on the hardwood before us and looking at me like I'm the biggest fool in the world. But he needn't have, because I was already calling myself that.

Boy, two dollars was a lot of money to pay for something that ended up tasting like sugar water, but I paid the freight, anyway.

Roxy drank hers right down in one gulp like she'd just crossed the desert and found the first watering hole.

"Another?" she said, her bosoms heaving.

I immediately thought of ol' Charley Utter.

"Sure," I said. "Go ahead and order. I need to use the jakes, I'll be right back."

Luckily Sam had drifted away after skinning me for those two dollars, I suppose to skin some others by gals like Roxy; it gave me time to escape and I went straight out the back door, past the jakes, and kept going.

The night air never felt so good; I did stink of cheap perfume and cigar smoke, but at least I still had most of the twenty dollars Albert and me had shared as part of the stage-line reward money, leaving the rest up in our hotel room. Albert thought it unwise to walk unfamiliar city streets with all that cash.

If the stars had at that moment all fallen out of the sky, I wouldn't have cared.

And just then, it felt like they had.

CHAPTER 8

I awoke to distant voices and a mangy hound licking my face.

"Ivory, Ivory," somebody was shouting at me through a tunnel.

My eyes fluttered open like window shades with bad roller springs.

At first, all I could see was watery images above me. Then something cold and wet hit my face and that finished the job up right good and I returned to the world of the living.

It was Albert and that big red-headed galoot what broke up the fight in the saloon earlier, and some others standing around gawking at me like I was some gink in a circus.

"Drat," said Albert, "I was worried you was croaked, scared the bejesus out of me, glad you're not."

"Makes two of us," I said, though it felt like someone was hammering inside my skull.

Sweet sour scents filled my nose. Turned out I was in a trashy alley, the same one I'd escaped into from the big harlot inside the saloon.

I sat up but not without paying the price. My entire head throbbed even harder and felt like it was cracked like that Liberty Bell I'd read about in the schoolbooks there at the orphanage.

The big red-headed fellow glared down at me with a questioning eye, and it was then was I saw the badge pinned to his shirt. How I missed it before I couldn't say. He didn't look any kinder or more compassionate than in the saloon when he threatened to shoot those fellows fighting.

"What happened to you, Nig?"

If I hadn't hurt so bad, I would have taken offense at him calling me Nig, but the way I was hurting just then he could have called me a three-legged dog and I wouldn't have cared.

"I don't know," I said shakily. "I just stepped out back to relieve myself and all went black until now."

"Old trick," said the lawman, chewing and spitting, a wad bulging in his cheek the size of a baseball. "You fancy boys come into town expecting romance for two, three dollars and this is what you get—screwed, but not the way you planned. Well, since you ain't dead and since you can't name the perpetrator of your assault, there's nothing I can do about it except say it's a lesson you done learned that will stick with you, and if not, then you are as dumb as you look, or not as smart, neither."

"Wait a minute," I said.

"What is it?" he growled.

"Are you the sheriff? Your deputy over at the jail said you were off somewheres."

He glanced around, then back at me with the look of someone who had just bit down on a stalk of rhubarb that wasn't ready to be eaten.

"No, I'm not the sheriff," he said, spitting again. "I'm the city marshal. Why, you writing a book on the laws in Cheyenne?"

Okay, so I was confused, but it angered me that the deputy at the jail hadn't been fully forthcoming about the law—like he was trying to run us off without assistance. Which I reckon is exactly what he'd done.

"Albert," I said, "show him that note."

Albert took out the piece of paper and showed it to the marshal, and he looked at it, then at me.

"So what?" he barked.

"Well, this is what the deputy at the jail gave us," Albert said.

The big man grunted and spat again till he almost had created a small brown puddle there on the ground by his boots.

"I reckon you two cockers is bound to get killed one way or t'other, but it ain't no concern of mine." Then he turned and strode off and others standing around gawping at me turned and followed him like a bunch of baby ducks after their ma. Except one man in a boiled white shirt and black claw-hammer coat with a flat-crowned black hat to match.

"Well what do you think of that?" Albert said to me. "Not real helpful, are they?"

"No, I reckon they ain't," I groaned.

Albert and the man in the white shirt helped me to my feet. I was still so woozy my legs felt like Chinese noodles in hot broth. Albert and White Shirt held me up till my balance returned and the world stopped spinning.

It was then I noticed my new boots are gone.

Not again!

And when I reached to touch the lump on the back of my head I asked Albert if my new hat was still up there.

"No, sorry, Ivory, it is not."

"Do you see it anywhere?"

"Nope."

Not again! It takes a low dog of a man to steal another man's boots and hat and I was starting to think that there were more low dogs in the town of Cheyenne than there were high ones.

Also, my pockets were turned out, but the thieves had failed to look under my shirt where I kept my money in the leather pouch tied around my neck. Still, I was beginning to feel like the biggest chump in the West.

"Name's Ambrose Bierce," White Shirt said, as they walked me out of the alley and into a nearby café and sat me down in a chair. The taste of hot black coffee helped clear my senses further. White shirt peered at me with colorless eyes through a pair of pince nez spectacles riding his long beak of a nose.

Then White Shirt took a calling card from the pocket of his brocade vest and, in so doing, revealed the small derringer poking out of the same vest pocket. He placed the card in front of me.

"Pinkerton operative, defunct," he said.

He seemed very proud of the *defunct* part, though, I don't know why.

"Means you're no longer," I said more for Albert's benefit before he could ask the question.

"Correct," White Shirt said.

"Why ain't you no longer a Pinkerton?" Albert asked.

"Seems I shot the wrong man—twice, for besmirching my reputation. And . . . I admit that being caught in the company of his vivacious wife might have had something to do with it, as well."

Even with a cloudy brain I couldn't help but wonder at the Pink's presence.

"Mr. Pettymoney?" I said, to which the Pink nodded.

"Indeed. I arrived early today at the behest of the banker. Went straightaway to the jail inquiring if they'd seen the likes of you two. And voilà! Here you are."

"But, if you're no longer a Pink?" Albert said.

"Matters not," said the Pink. "I pulled the assignment just before I shot the gentleman in question. The shooting scrape is yet unknown back at the home office, so, let's keep it that way, all right, boys?"

I didn't take it as a request so much as I did a threat.

"Well, I appreciate you offering to help Albert and me," I said.

"What are we if not our brother's keeper?" he replied and

gave me a wolfish grin.

"That's from the Bible," Albert said, quite pleased with his scope of knowledge from that particular source, but I found nothing holy in it the way it came out of the Pink's mouth.

"Wonders never cease," I said in a foul mood.

"It's good I caught up to you boys when I did," Pink said.

"Well, thanks again," I said, in order to shoo him off. But he didn't shoo easily for he refused to take the hint and scat. So, for a time, we drank our coffee in meditation and he smoked a black cheroot. But for the scraping of spoons on cups and saucers as well as being surrounded by the chatter of other diners who chirped and carried on like caged parakeets, but maybe not as smart. It was a den of solitude.

"Mr. Bierce here says he's an expert at finding folks that don't want to be found, Ivory," Albert informed me.

"How was it you two met?" I asked.

"Like I said, Ivory," Albert replied. "Mr. Bierce here is an expert at finding folks, ain't that so, Mr. Bierce?"

At which the Pink nodded and dabbed his lips with a napkin and I noticed when he did, he had no dirt or grime under his fingernails like so many of them professional manslayers, which often as not come in the form of self-described *detectives* that might just as easily be classified as killers for hire.

"That's right," Pink stated. "I'm a Jim-doodle-dandy at finding folks, and I aim to find One-eye Texas Jack Crowfoot and his bunch. Now don't you two worry none, Mr. Pettymoney has requested that I tell you that your friend Gus got a right proper burial. Say, can I ask you boys something?"

Albert nodded. I just held my sore head feeling around the goose egg growing out of my skull.

"Sure," said Albert.

"Why in the world would you want your dead pard to have a window put into the lid of his coffin?"

Albert looked at me, but I didn't bother looking back.

"Case somebody wanted to look in," he said rather weakly. "I reckon is why."

"Oh, you mean, they'd have to dig him up first to look in so they could see him. I got that about right?"

You didn't have to be a genius to hear the amusement in the Pink's tone. He was stirring our beans and I wasn't needing my beans stirred.

"That's right!" I growled to let him know I ain't playing and I don't much appreciate his taking such a tone with us. Sure, he seemed learned and mannered enough, but maybe that was the problem as I saw it. He thought me and Albert to be young rubes, country bumpkins just fallen off the hay wagon, on account of we're young still. Sister Mary Virgin taught me never to judge a book by its cover and I was doing my best not to judge this Pink, but he wasn't making it easy. I knew after she went off with that man in the buggy, she was right. I'd judged her as pure and innocent only to learn that maybe she was not as pure and innocent as I'd been led to believe. Another thing she'd said once was that still waters run deep. I'm still working on figuring that one out.

Mr. Ambrose Bierce simply chuckled like I'd told him a nice little joke that could be told in mixed company, like why did the rooster cross the road, and then come up with some corny answer: "Oh, to get to the other side." Titter, titter.

"Now listen, gents, I've done a lot of research in the agency's files on these birds, and I've come up with one possible location of this here Robbers Roost. And from what I can tell, it's just as advertised, a roost for banditti." He paused long enough to let that sink in, or, if you will, to lord his fine education over us.

"Bandits, you mean?" said Albert right smartly. I felt my efforts at passing on my knowledge of Mr. Webster's book to Albert well worth every syllable just then.

"Well, now," Pink came back, "I bet you were so bright your pappy called you son." Gave us that smart-alecky smile.

"His pap's dead, mister," I said. "So, best you leave off with any further talk about him."

The Pink turned a marble-like eye on me and I thought, *we ain't going to get along so good.*

He drummed his fingers atop the table, one of which flashed a gold pinkie ring with a ruby and he caught me staring at it.

"Looks like a drop of blood, don't it?" he said proudly. "It belonged to none other than John Wesley Hardin. I purchased it in a Dallas pawnshop. The owner said he sold it to help pay his attorney's expenses when they were trying him for murdering Texas police, most of which had the same color of skin as you, Ivory. The story goes, in fact, that the gold in this ring was extracted from the teeth of some of those murdered police. But who is to really say?"

"He probably would like it back," I said.

"Oh, I just bet he would. But it would do him little good up in the state pen where he's serving twenty-five years. Why I'm willing to wager had he slain so many police—Negro or no—in any other state he'd be worm food by now. But Texas, well, they got their own kind of justice."

"I need to go lay down," I said. "My head's busting."

"Sure, sure. Heard you boys was staying at the hotel. What's say I swing by in the morning and we'll together cobble a plan?"

Without so much as waiting for an answer the Pink got up and strolled out. The lowering sun coming through the dusty café window like it was caused my pain to feel like somebody was running a hot iron through my brain.

"Listen, Ivory. You want me to walk you on over to the hotel?" Albert asked.

"Why, where are you headed?" I said.

"Oh, Geneva, Ginny, has invited me for dinner at her place. I was thinking maybe later this evening asking her for a moonlight stroll. Her uncle Brick seems really nice too."

"That's the way you're going to do me, huh? Soon as some pretty gal comes along and bats her eyes, you drop ol' Ivory here like second-grade arithmetic?"

I know I shouldn't have said it soon as the words left my mouth, but the pain was messing with my thinking.

"I'm sorry," I said. "It's just the pain talking. You go on. I can make it back okay. I'll be better after I get some rest, a little nap maybe and I'll be fit as a five-legged dog."

"Are you sure?" Albert said, a concerned look on his face.

I waved a hand for him to go on. But to show him there really weren't any hard feelings on my part I asked an inquiry of him.

"Say, how'd that opera turn out, anyway?"

He scowled.

"Why it was just a bunch of fat people running around bellering and brandishing fake swords and pretend fighting," he said. "I couldn't make heads or tails of it. But don't tell Geneva I said that, she'll think I'm an ignoramus."

"Why, Albert, I thought you was, ain't you?" I said with my best effort to grin.

He grinned back.

"Okay, I'll see you later at the hotel," he said and hurried off.

"See you," I said and watched him happily go, and truth was, I was happy for him as well, for I do believe that is what being friends is about, one being happy for another's happiness just as when they are sad.

CHAPTER 9

So, there I sat, bareheaded and bootless, ruminating how sideways things had gone since last we laid eyes on our old pard, Gus Monroe, stiff as a board and powdered up like a two-dollar hussy waiting for a paramour to come along. Boy howdy.

Now Albert's gone and gotten moon-eyed on a gal older than him and good looking to boot. I just can't figure what her interest is in him other than his good nature. But maybe she's like that old lady's cow back in Last Whisky that was never content on just eating the grass on its side of the fence and had to stick its head through the barbed wire to get at the other side and would get stuck and have the old lady's man come along and unstuck it, all the while cussing a blue streak and saying "What's wrong with you, you can't learn not to stick your head through this dang fence, you think the grass on the other side is better?" And sometimes to get his point across, the old lady's man would smack the cow with a board.

I just hoped Geneva, or Ginny as he'd taken to calling her, didn't go and break his heart bone, for she seemed to me a woman much capable of breaking men's heart bones as any I'd ever seen. Had that sweetness about her that would draw a feller to her like flies to honey. I'm not saying I wouldn't have been just the same as my friend had she turned them eyes on me instead. I probably would.

Nothing to do but head back to the hotel and try and sleep, hoping the pain would make its way out of my head like a thief in the night. I reasoned my head wasn't going to get any better just setting there with folks staring at me, a hatless, bootless colored kid with a goose egg growing out of my head.

By the time I got to the hotel and up to my room, the pain was so awful I felt like I was going to go blind. But I managed to shuck out of my duds and ease down onto the feather bed and let my eyes gratefully close, and even that felt like rusty gears turning in my brain.

I don't know what happened after that, but I was awakened by somebody knocking at the door. And, at first, I thought maybe I was just dreaming that somebody was knocking at the door, considering what awful things can happen once you've had your eggs scrambled.

It was dark both within and without my room when I glanced through the window, and I couldn't rightly tell if night had fallen or morning was coming.

"Albert? That you?" I managed to get out of my poor mouth. No answer.

Knock, knock.

"Albert, if'n that's you, please go away and let me rest some more."

Knock, knock, knock.

Much to my regret, I eased out of bed wearing just my union suit and instantly got so dizzy I almost fell down, but grabbed onto the bed until the room stopped spinning.

Knock, knock, knock.

"Hold on, I'm trying to get there!"

And, finally, I staggered to the door and cracked it open.

"Albert, that you?"

Of a sudden, the face of Jazzy appeared before me and I knew I was dreaming. But the gas jets in the hall told me I wasn't, for she was real.

"Fool let me in, don't make me stand out here in this

hallway," she said as if agitated. So, I stepped aside and in she came trailing an air of sweet scent behind her. Once in, she asked me: "You a bat?"

"Huh?"

"It's dark as a cave in here. Light a lamp a'fore I trip over somethin' and bust my leg."

I remembered there was an oil lamp on a stand by the bed, matches to light it with. I fumbled around until I struck a flame that glowed like a promise inside the soot-crusted glass chimney and filled the room with greasy warm light, but, with Jazzy in the room the light seemed more romantic.

"What are you doing here?" I asked.

She looked at me with those big brown wet eyes.

"What? You don't want me here? Well I can just turn right around and leave, then," she said in a false pout.

I quick grabbed for my shirt and trousers draped over the back of a chair, but she stopped me from doing so.

"Why you want to get dressed, and I just got here? Don't you want me here, Ivory?"

"Well, of course I do," I said. "I'm just surprised, and delighted, don't forget that part," if you understand how it is with a teenage boy who is almost a man.

She had started unbuttoning her dress and stepped out of her shoes while letting the dress fall down around her feet, the whole time gazing straight into my eyes.

So, I told her what happened to me and how Albert found me and I had my hat and boots swiped yet again and leaned over to show her the knot on my head, which she then proceeded to delicately kiss and whisper a whole lot of nice things to me and, law, but I started feeling miraculously better.

"Your friend Albert said I could find you here," she whispered just standing in her lacy bloomers. She was looking so mighty fine that way my injury seemed like something I might have read about in a dime book, like maybe it was Buffalo Bill hit over the head and not yours truly.

Then she started to work on my buttons, of which there ain't that many on a union suit. I didn't try and stop her, or stammer any kind of objection since she seemed to know what she was doing. Then when she had the task just about complete and it was just me and nothing else standing there, she kissed me full on the mouth.

"You like that Ivory?" she said when she pulled back.

"Uh-huh."

"You want to kiss me back?"

"Uh-huh."

"Well?"

So, I kissed her back and then she kissed my kiss back, and pretty soon her tongue is darting in and out of my mouth and mine starts darting till it's like we're playing sword fighting with our tongues while our hands are searching each other's bodies like one of us had hid something the other is intent on finding. Hers was smooth as satin and round and she cooed like a mourning dove and a pigeon talking to each other on a fence in the evenings.

Then she led me to the bed in the most proper improper way I've ever been led anywhere, and gladly let myself be thus led and would again a thousand times over. She sure seemed to know what it was I wanted.

We set on the side of the bed and kept on kissing and holding each other until finally we took a little break so we could catch our breaths. My heart was kicking inside my chest like a snared rabbit.

"How are you feeling now, Ivory?" she asked, lightly running her fingertips up over my head.

"Let's just say if you was a doctor or a traveling preacher, I'd done be healed. And everywhere you been touching me, I'm also healed even though I wasn't rightly knowing I was hurting in such places. You go on and keep touching case somebody hits me over the head again later."

She laughed and hugged me tightly.

"How come you're not at the café?" I said.

"Why, they ain't open this hour no more."

"What time is it?"

"Oh, it's around nine o'clock."

"Oh, I done fell asleep when I got back here."

"You sure you all right, honey?" she asked still hugging me.

"Yes'm. I'm more than all right."

Laughter again.

"I can see that you are," she said, letting her hand drop down to my lap.

But I'm nervous and don't know what exactly I should do next, whether she wants more of what we've been doing, or less now that we'd taken a break from doing it and maybe she was thinking I'm completely healed.

"You want to go for a walk somewhere or something?" I said, not sure what else to say in that wanting moment.

"Or something," she said and started trying to find all those other aching parts of me with her delicate fingers and hands as she laid me back on the bed with her beside me.

Then we proceeded to do I guess what we were there to do, what the Lord put in us to do, one with the other, and it was all natural like and wonderful in so many ways and a dang sight better than a walk. And even as we were doing it, I thought someday I'd write about it, which I'm doing now because all this happened some years ago. But not so old I can't remember it like it was just this morning. I don't reckon no matter how old a body gets it still remembers certain things just as it forgets other things.

Well, when Jazzy finished with me and me with her, I felt like

I'd been caught in a furious storm of pure pleasure if there was such a thing. All wrung out and weak, too. But Jazzy was all spirited still, and got up and got dressed and kissed me one last time and said she had to get going and it seemed at that point she was in a real hurry to get on.

"I was wondering if you might just want to stay here tonight with me. The room's all paid for another day, and it's dark and late and who knows who might try and molest you out on them streets." I tried not to make it sound like I was begging, but that is exactly what I was doing.

"Oh, that's sweet of you to offer, Ivory, but I can't stay. My husband be off his job at the railroad and be waiting for me and wonderin' why I'm late. And besides, I had all the molesting a gal can hope for in one night."

Husband!

She blew me a kiss and was out the door before I could get over my startlement. By the time I got myself dressed and down the stairs and on out into the street, there was just a row of gaslights that seemed to add a keen loneliness to the night, and no sign of her anywhere. Gone, quick as a hare. I was instantly reminded of what Mr. Utter had said in the saloon about lonesomeness.

I stood there wondering if I wasn't the biggest fool in the world. I just couldn't believe Jazzy was married. She looked so young and pert. But maybe those were the very reasons that she *was* married, for what man wouldn't want a gal like her in his bed every night and his kitchen every day? And to make matters worse, my head was throbbing again.

Then, before I could come to reason with what had just occurred, here come Albert hurrying up the street.

"Ivory!"

"What?"

"Ivory!"

143

"What?"

"Ivory!"

"What is it, Albert, is you snakebit or something?" For he looked like maybe a snake had gotten him and he knew he only had a few minutes yet to live. I once knew a boy got bitten by a big rattler on his way home to supper and he was dead by the time he finished a plate of sweet potatoes and ham. He had the same look on his face as that on Albert's: all twisted up and horrified.

When Albert got up to me, he bent over at the waist and put his hands on his knees and was breathing hard like he couldn't catch his breath.

"What is wrong with you?" I said again. "Is the poison running through your body?"

He held out an arm as if to allow for patience, then slowly straightened up and was hardly able to look me in the eyes, but when he finally did, I saw the most wounded look as I've seen on anyone.

"You ain't going to believe what happened," he huffed.

"Oh, so you know, then?"

"Know what?"

"About Jazzy and me—up in the room? She said you told her how to find me, and she sure enough found me. Was you outside the door listening, is that how you know?"

"What are you talking about, Ivory? I swear you confound me." Then: "No! It ain't nothing to do about you and Jazzy . . . Wait, you saying you and she?"

I nodded.

"Like a pair of rabid rabbits," I said. "But that ain't even the worst of it."

"Worst of it?" Now he looked truly confounded.

"She told me right afterwards that she was a married woman

and run off home to her husband. Lord almighty, I feel besmirched!"

He expelled a great breath of air.

"Ivory," he said with slow impatience. I knew that look so well I explained it.

"Means sullied." He stilled looked at me blankly, so I add: "Tarnished, or dirty," to which he simply shook his head.

"Well, I'm sorry for you," he said. "But if anyone is to feel *besearched* it's me. No, Ivory, it ain't about you and Jazzy. It's about what happened when I was over at Ginny's."

"Did you and she . . . ?"

"Oh gawd!" he cried so loud I thought everybody in the hotel would hear him.

"I'm listening, Albert," though I was only half listening on account of still suffering my own shock.

"Well, we all sat down to eat, including, of course, her uncle, and had a real nice supper and things were going along swell. Then Uncle Brick said he was going on to bed and would leave Ginny and me to ourselves. Said, 'Now, you two kids don't do nothing I wouldn't.' Where have I heard that before? So fine, and me and Ginny go on in the living room and sit on the couch and she starts kissing and loving on me and so I start doing the same thing to her."

"Is this going to take awhile?" I said, for Albert is no natural-born storyteller and my head was still buzzing with the thought that any minute Jazzy's husband was going to show up irate and with a gun.

"Just listen," Albert demanded. "So, next thing I know she leads me into her bedroom and it all happened so quick I couldn't believe it."

"The lovemaking?" I said. "Why Albert, I am proud of you."

"Don't be," he groaned. "It was what happened before the lovemaking part. And you know, I'm just going along with whatever she is having me do even though I never was with no girl before, but figure it will come to me, and Ginny sure enough seemed knowledgeable in the ways of the world."

"Albert, please, I'm about to pass out, hurry it along."

He gave me one of his ghastly looks like he does when he is displeased with me.

"I'm getting there."

I nod to let him know to go on.

"Well there we are rassling around on the bed, naked as sin itself when what happens, but Uncle Brick shows up, also naked, and says something like, 'Now, ain't this just a sight' and starts to get in bed with us. I about jumped so high I dang near hit the ceiling thinking Ginny's gonna start hollering for him to get out. But she don't. Instead, they start cooing at each other and telling me to relax. Well you can see how much I relaxed on account I'm standing here telling you about this. I swear, Ivory, them two is perverted."

Albert flopped over at the waist again and started gagging.

"Have you even ever heard of such a thing?" he gasped.

"Not personally, no."

"I swear, if I had some dang liquor I'd drink it down straight out of the bottle," Albert said. "Then I'd go back over there and punch him in the nose."

"What about her?" I asked.

"What do you mean, what about her?" Albert said.

"I mean she was as much a part of it as Uncle Brick."

This he considered a moment as we stood under the greasy yellow eye of the gaslight.

"I reckon you're right," he said forlornly. "I just never thought about hitting a woman. More'n that, though, it breaks my heart she turned out like she did."

"You remember Otero, don't you?"

"That Mexican bought you from the orphanage? Why sure I

146

do. All he did was sit around drinking that tequila and watched you work building them coffins."

"That's right," I said. "But aside from teaching me to carpenter, he also taught me a lot about life. Said when he was a young bandit he had probably made love to a thousand women and said he enjoyed them all even though he ended up having to shoot a few. And when I asked him why he shot them, he merely laughed and said they needed shooting and that there were plenty more fishes in the sea."

Albert looked at me dumbly.

"I don't get your point."

"His, not mine. But what he meant and a good lesson you need to learn right now: there will be other gals for you down the line. She's not the first, and she'll likely not be your last. And best of all, you don't even have to shoot her."

He stood for a moment, then laughed.

"I could, the way I'm feeling."

"No, you couldn't, Albert. You ain't that way."

"You're right," he said.

"See, there," I said. "Let's get a good night's sleep and see what tomorrow brings."

"What about going in search of this Chink Town and finding them Pallor brothers?"

"We may not require their services now that Banker Pettymoney's Pink has arrived. He might be all we need."

"Maybe so," Albert agreed. "I let myself get all twisted around over that gal and her crazy uncle. I knew it was too good to be true."

"Live and learn," I said.

"Don't count your chickens before they hatch."

"Easy come, easy go."

"One hand washes the other."

"What?"

"Never mind, forget it, I'm going back to bed."

"Me too."

And so, we slept, Albert alone in his room and me in the arms of Morpheus and all his hideous dreams about an irate husband with a loaded shotgun barging into the room looking for his wife's paramour. Calling my name in the long dark: "Ivory! Ivory Cade! What you do with my woman, Ivory Cade? I aim to murder you over it."

"Ivory ain't here," a disembodied voice answers.

CHAPTER 10

The Pink, Ambrose Bierce, was waiting for us in the lobby the next morning. He looked like a killer looking for somebody to kill, with his wide black belt and two black holsters and two guns strapped around the outside of his gray suit. Otherwise, he could have as easily passed for a parson.

"Mornin', lads."

We exchanged brief pleasantries.

"Well, I've some bad news," he informed us. "I must head immediately to Missouri in pursuit of the James gang who have robbed yet another train."

"But you said you were defunct as far as being a Pink," Albert said.

"Am," Bierce replied, lighting a cheroot he took from a little silver box and off which he struck a wood match to light the cheroot with; then he puffed two or three times, snapped out the match, and dropped it into one of several fancy knee-high ashtrays there in the lobby.

"But I'm a voracious reader of newspapers and having read of the robberies, I know that the Pinkertons are in hot pursuit," Bierce further explained. "I figure if I can locate these rascals before my former companions, I stand a fair chance of making a lot more than a couple of hundred dollars working for Pettymoney. Besides, I think that is now a lost cause at this stage of the game. Even if we could have gotten her back, I doubt that man would want her knowing the indignities visited upon the poor woman by now."

"That so," I said getting mad at the man. "So, you just shirk your responsibilities for a bigger score?"

He looked at me with one squinted eye against the rising smoke of his stogie and grinned.

"You're a quick learner, Ivory. It's all about economics in my business. So long, it's been good to meetcha!" And with that he turned, carrying his leather case, and headed out, no doubt, in time to catch the next train for Missouri, a place I know very little about, but for the infamy of the brothers Frank and Jesse James, of whom I read are from the Little Dixie section in the western reaches of that state.

"Do you think it might be something about us," Albert asked, "that soon as we get someone to hook up with us they up and leave in a hurry?"

I truly didn't know, but had my suspicions.

"It might be more about the mission than about us, Albert."

"A fool's journey, then?"

"I refuse to look at it that way. I think about that woman and what she must be suffering at the hands of that devil One-eye Texas Jack, and the only thing that can save her now is us, Albert."

He looked unconvinced.

"Oh, oh," I said.

"What is it?"

"There's a big black bruiser headed this way and he's armed with a shotgun."

Albert spun around to stare out the windows.

"Where?" he said.

I laughed.

"Made you look!"

"Dang it all, Ivory."

"Come'n, let's go see if we can find this Chink Town."

Albert halted me and pointed at my feet, which were bare, and then at my head, still sore, but also bare.

"You will need boots and a hat," he said.

"Oh, yeah," I said.

"Let's get you kitted out, then find this place," Albert proposed.

"Say, why don't we ask him if he knows where this Chink Town is?" I pointed to the desk clerk. "Seems a feller works in a hotel ought to know where everything is in town."

I think between whoever coldcocked me and my time with Jazzy my brains were as scrambled as breakfast eggs.

So that's what we did and the clerk said, "Sure, it's across the tracks, other side of town. Where they do a lot of laundering, and if you're so inclined, where you can buy yourself a turn with the pipe."

"Pipe?" I said.

"Opium dens. There is two or three over there."

And, of course, neither Albert nor myself knew what an opium den was and the clerk explained that it is a place to smoke opium, which led to more confusion on Albert's part.

"Don't you boys know nothing?" the clerk said smugly when he saw the quizzical look on Albert's mug. Me, I try and act like I know things I don't just so I don't end up looking clueless.

Before Albert could speak and make us sound even more like rubes, I piped up and said, "Shoot, we're not much inclined to such things, mister. Maybe you are but me and Albert here is good Christians whose ma taught us to lead a righteous life that don't include smoking opium or anything else. Ain't that right, Albert?"

"Or fooling around with women and their perverted uncles, neither," Albert blurted out unnecessarily, which confused the clerk.

"They stay to themselves, them people," the clerk said. "You can get just about anything you want over there that you can't get here on this side of the tracks." The clerk pointed with his bony finger in the direction he was referring to, then added: "To be forewarned is to be forearmed."

"What's that supposed to mean?" I said.

"Nothing," he said "I just like saying it."

"What wouldn't you do?" Albert asked.

"Not a thing I can conjure," Mr. Smart Aleck clerk said and grinned, showing us how much in need of a dentist he was.

Albert reminded me again I needed new boots and a hat or I'd look like a dolt going around barefoot and bareheaded.

"You're right," I said. "I would look worse than a dolt. But this is the last time. I'll shoot the next guttersnipe who tries taking my foot and headwear."

So, we made a quick trip back to Mister Snooty where we purchased before but soon as we entered, his smart mouth said: "You boys come back for your old clothes? Sorry, but I burned them." Then he hooted like a schoolgirl at what he considered his own joke, but wasn't. Albert and me mostly ignored him and I picked a hat and another pair of boots that smelled of fresh leather.

"You lads sure run though things, don't you," he said.

"Wouldn't if there wasn't a bunch of boot and hat thieves in this town," I said, tugging on the new pair. They were low heeled and square toed and no fancy stitching, which suited me just fine.

We paid him and then headed over to the livery to pick up our horses, which looked rested and well fed and sleek as seals. After we saddled them and loaded our gear on, we walked them across the tracks until we caught the scent of cooking and came in view of Celestials mingling in front of stores with strange writing I reckoned is their English instead of our own; and inside storefronts and right out on the walks, they were also selling food.

"Look," said Albert, pointing at a window front with a hanging row of plucked ducks.

"Seems mighty gruesome," I said.

A small Chinese fellow the color of candle wax approached, and in spotty lingo asked if we want to, "Buy duck?"

"No," I said. "But we're looking for two fellows goes by the name of Pallor? You heard of them?"

"Pallor? Oh, yes, yes, you come," and he crooked a finger for us to follow and we went down one street, then another, and turned into an alley, all of which made me skittish on account of the last time I found myself in an alley wasn't none too pleasant. But since it was morning and I had Albert with me, I followed along, but with a hand resting on the butt of my new used Schofield pistol, so felt a might easier about it.

Finally, he stopped at a door and opened it and crooked his finger again to follow him in.

"What do you think, Ivory?" Albert said.

"Keep your gun handy," I said.

Well, anyway, inside there was nothing but cots with men lying on them and either holding or puffing on what looked like clarinets with little bowls on top. The room was swirling with fog-like smoke and smelled pungent.

"Best not breathe in too deeply," I said to Albert.

" 'At's pretty interesting smell, ain't it?" Albert said.

Then the old man led us over to a set of cots and lying across each were what looks like twins, only they were as white a' fellows as I have ever seen in my life. I mean more white than your average white man by a sight.

"See, see," the old Chinese said, pointing at them. "Pallas."

"They look like they're dreaming, only they're eyes ain't fully shut," Albert said.

I agreed, then suggested we wait outside for them.

"We stay in here much longer and we'll end up like them," I said. So, we went outside and waited in the alley, squatting down on our heels and holding the reins of our horses.

We waited a long time and Albert asked me why them fellows are so white and I remembered a boy back at the orphanage was that way and Sister Mary Virgin told me he was an Albino. Had pink eyes and white nappy hair like mine, only mine is black. So I told Albert they are called Albinos.

He repeated the word so as to get a taste of it.

"Well, where do they come from, Ivory, these Albinos?"

I shrugged and said, "All over, I reckon. The sister at the orphanage I told you about before was the one what explained it to me, said it was just a rare thing. But you know something? That kid, Zeno, was his name, I do recall. Nobody much got around him. He was always off by himself. Then one day they found him dead in his bunk. Just like that. Almost like he had prayed for it."

Again, I recalled what Colorado Charley Utter had said about lonesomeness and all its many forms. I hadn't considered it at the time, but now I did.

Albert sat quiet for a minute, then shook his head slowly.

"That's sure a sad tale, Ivory."

"Ain't it, though."

After what seemed a long, long time, out they came, the two Albinos, and I don't reckon from the way they was armed—each wearing a pair of revolvers along with a butcher knife tucked into their belt—nobody was likely to give them any grief.

They looked down at Albert and me with their red eyes just as we got up from squatting there, my knees cracking like dry twigs, and I wondered what they'd be like when they turned old age, say forty.

" 'Scuse us," I said. "Are you two fellers the Pallor brothers?"

"Who's asking?" one of them said. You couldn't tell one from the other so much alike were they.

"Show 'em the note that deputy wrote," I said to Albert who took it out and handed it to them.

"Chink Town, huh?" the fellow said after reading it and grinned. He had short blunted teeth white as pearls.

"That's what he wrote, yessir," I said.

"Well, why is it you are asking about us?" the other one said.

"We're after a gang of outlaws who robbed a bank and kidnapped the banker's wife and he's offering a reward," I said. I didn't want to, but I didn't know how else to bait the hook, for they struck me as serious types who wouldn't walk across the street if you asked them without offering them something. I also figured that the deputy must have considered them serious types as well or he wouldn't have written down their names.

"Yeah, what sort of reward?" they said in unison.

"Five hundred dollars. We'll split it fifty-fifty if you'll take us to this place called the Robbers Roost and help us get Tittey back," Albert said before I could stop him.

"Tittey?" one said.

I explained how it was the banker's pet name for his wife whose real name was Antietam.

"That so?" one said.

"Two hundred and change don't seem like much, considering we're riding into the Robbers Roost," the other said.

"Real bad place if you ain't one of them," the first one said.

"Real bad, especially for Albinos," the second one said. "Once the killing starts, and it will start, it don't matter who we kill."

"Let us confer," they said.

Albert and me waited while they walked up the alley a bit and murmured their thoughts, one to the other, then returned.

"Okay, we agree to your terms," the one said and held out his hand and I went to shake on it but he withdrew and said, "Pay up front."

"Won't have it until after Mrs. Pettymoney is found and I can wire her husband and have him in turn wire the money right here to the bank."

This news didn't seem to please him much.

"Sounds like a ruse," the other one said.

So, right there, I stopped them and asked them to tell me who was who because I was confused and one said, "You see how his ears stick out farther than mine?" pointing at the other one.

"Yes, I see now that you point it out," I said. I hadn't noticed before, because like I said, it gave me the spooks to stare at them very long.

"Well, that tells you I'm Wallace and my brother here is Alonzo."

"How do we know you can even get the money?" Alonzo asked and not in a very friendly manner.

"We can send a wire to Mister Pettymoney to confirm," Albert said. Boy, he often surprised me with his quick mind at times.

"Let us confer," Wallace said and he and his brother once more walked off a bit to talk among themselves.

"Thanks, Ivory," Albert said. "I know we'll be in the hole at best on this deal, but at least we can go home again, which is something poor Gus can't ever say."

"Way I look at it," I said, "we never did have much and probably never going to have much, but our dignity. Least we got that."

Though what I was thinking was that we might fail in our mission and end up as dead as Gus and no going home for either of us.

Wallace and Alonzo returned.

"Tell you what, we'll take your terms and if you don't come up with the money once the job is done and we get back here,

156

we'll kill you both and keep the woman for ourselves," Alonzo said.

Well, talk about a heart stopper.

"Normally we work cash, gold or silver, not script," Wallace said.

"But the costs of chasing the dragon is not cheap," said Alonzo.

"More expensive than whores," Wallace said.

"A lot more," Alonzo said.

"You boys ever chased the dragon?" Wallace said.

"No, sir," Albert said. I seconded Albert's reply.

"Where do you find this dragon, anyway?" Albert said.

Both of them grinned, showing their red gums and pearl-like teeth.

"Inside," Wallace said.

"You mean smoking that opium," I said.

"You're a fast study, darkie," Alonzo said.

"Well, don't start if you ain't," Wallace said.

"So we were forewarned," I said.

"By the hotel clerk," Albert said.

"Well let's get started if we're going to kill some people," Alonzo said.

"All this standing around talking is making my skin itch," Wallace said.

"The dragon awaits!" declared Alonzo, and Wallace grinned.

"So, you know where the Robbers Roost is, then?" Albert said.

"Of course, we do," Wallace said.

"We know where every low den of iniquity in the territory is," Alonzo said.

"But mostly we know where every opium den is, that's what really matters," Wallace said.

Albert and I exchanged glances.

"We're hoping we don't have to kill anybody, that we can just kidnap Mrs. Pettymoney back," I said.

I don't know what it was but they both started laughing. And when they finally stopped they gave us those red-eye stares.

"You children best take cover then," Alonzo said. "Let me and Wallace handle the killing."

"We sort of get a kick out of plugging folks that need it, ain't that right, Alonzo?"

"There is bound to be killing," Wallace said.

"Bound to be," his brother confirmed.

"But not to worry, it's what we're good at, Wallace and me, killing," Alonzo said.

"We can hold our own," Albert piped up, and I know why he did but wished he hadn't.

"No doubt," Alonzo said, and they started laughing again and poking one another in the ribs like children.

Though they were both dressed completely in black, that made them seem even whiter than they were, and both wore fancy leather gun belts with hand-tooled holsters from which protruded ivory-handled revolvers, I thought them either crazy or extremely dangerous, but at least they dressed nice.

Exactly the type we needed to go after One-eye Texas Jack Crowfoot.

CHAPTER 11

We followed the Pallor brothers over to the livery where they'd kept their horses, both of which were as black as their clothing and snorting and prancing about like the devil's own.

I asked Albert in a low voice what he thought while we waited for them to saddle the beasts.

"They're scary," he said back in as low a voice.

"I think so too. Imagine going up against them," I said.

"I can't. I can't imagine trying to even with my gun and they was holding a slingshot on me."

"Me, either."

"You think they're as dangerous as they appear?" Albert said, still in a low voice.

"More," I said.

"No, I mean do you wonder if they're dangerous enough to handle One-eye and help us get Mrs. Pettymoney, then kill the two of us and keep her?"

"Couldn't say. Maybe."

"I'm not sure I like it."

"The die is cast," I said, having read that in a book and always looked for chances to use it.

Albert looked at me as if I'd just told him I saw Jesus tending bar at some saloon.

There was something in the way they moved, almost catlike, as if afraid to step too hard on the ground like felines, in that they seemed not to have any bones to restrict their movement.

When they finished saddling their mounts and climbed aboard and me and Albert climbed aboard ours, they headed off in a westerly direction and Albert and me followed along behind till about noon when we spelled the horses and ourselves. It was awfully hot with the sun beating down and the Pallor brothers said they needed to get in the shade for a while on account of their skin being so pale. So, we took a respite under some cottonwoods. I thought to make conversation in a way that would incline them toward Albert and me in case things went sideways when we got to this Robbers Roost.

"Where you fellows hail from?" I said, mostly to try and warm up to their company if you know what I mean. I didn't know how those Albinos thought, or what they thought of. I wondered, too, if there were Albino women, or how all that worked out. Sometimes I think I think too much, and Albert has told me the same.

"All over, mostly," Wallace said.

Alfonzo's red eyes seemed to be scouring everything around him like maybe he was one of those creatures that are always looking for something to kill. Predators, I think they are called.

"We're man hunters," Wallace said. "Man hunting takes you here, there, and everywhere, so that there is no one place we're from. Don't mean to sound rude about it, just thought I'd clarify."

"I see," I said.

"You like that sort of work, do you?" Albert piped up.

Now both the brothers' red eyes took in Albert and I was just as glad it was him than me having all four eyes staring at you like that.

"Like it a lot," Wallace said. "Ain't that right, Alonzo?"

"We do," Alonzo said. "We don't have nobody telling us what to do or when to do it. We can work if we want or not work. Gives us lots of time to chase the dragon."

"And whores," Wallace added.

"And whores," Alonzo confirmed.

So, you could see how I might have been thinking about if there were such as Albino women, or did the Albino men go for regular ones. But then I thought what does the regular ones feel about Albino men?

"What about you two?" Alonzo asked. "You wanting to be man hunters, or just out on a lark trying to get this Tittey woman back to her husband?"

"Oh, we're just regular boys out of Last Whisky original," Albert said. "We're not real man hunters such as you two. Well, I guess in the purest sense of the word, we are presently, yes."

"But this is an exception for Albert and me," I added.

"It's just that this particular fellow, Texas Jack, killed a friend of our'n before he and his gang robbed the bank and stole the woman. Otherwise we'd probably be home fishing and skipping school maybe," Albert said.

"Or gigging frogs and shooting marbles," I add.

This set them to laughing again, but I can't say as to why. It seemed pretty common what we said, nothing funny in it. And when they stopped laughing Alonzo hooted: "Gigging frogs!"

Which then prompted Wallace to jump in.

"Well, sonny, gigging frogs is a lot different than gigging men, ain't it so, Alonzo?"

"And they don't taste as good, neither," Alonzo said, and this started a whole new round of laughter.

"Don't taste as good!" Wallace snorted.

Finally, we got back on the trail again and as we rode along, I was feeling even more unnerved by our new companions and wondered if we hadn't made a mistake in offering to split the reward money. Then, too, the thought struck me that the reason that deputy gave us their names was in order to rid the town of the entire bunch of us in one fell swoop without having to fire a shot.

By eventide we came to a place that looked little more than a long low cabin and the Pallor brothers reined in and we did too.

"Get us some grub here, rest the horses overnight, leave out in the morning," Wallace said.

Neither Albert or me were about to argue. My backside was sore and my legs cramping. The sun had gone low beyond some hills and spread the land with a rosy light. Mourning doves cooed off in the chaparral as they tended to do while dusting themselves come evening.

Alonzo, or maybe it was Wallace—I couldn't be sure in the failing light—knocked on the door and a woman who looked like a witch answered. She was maybe the tallest woman I'd ever seen. She was so tall she had to stoop down to see out.

"Two Bits!" she yelled to someone inside. "Git out here, we got company."

"Well holy Mary and Joseph!" he yelped and clapped his hands. "I guess it ain't true after all."

"What ain't true," Alonzo said (at least I think it was Alonzo).

"Heard they killed you boys over in New Mexico. Some sheriff's posse," Clubfoot said.

"That'll be the day," one of the Pallor brothers said as they pushed inside the cabin.

The witch woman stared out at Albert and me.

"I see you boys brought something for the cook pot," she said in a cackling voice.

"You better get on in here," one of the Pallor brothers called, "else she's liable to chop you up and feed you to the next ones come along."

So, in we went as the clubfoot came out and took our horses saying, "Don't worry, don't worry, that ol' bitch is just jaking you."

We went in and set around a long pine table the brothers were already seated at and filling their plates from a steaming cauldron of some sort of brown gravy stew with chunks of meat, and helping themselves to a platter of yeasty smelling biscuits. There was a pot of coffee and a pitcher of buttermilk. You would have thought you'd set down in some low-run hotel dining room rather than a cabin.

Albert and me followed suit while the witch woman kept moving about, muttering under her breath senselessly like a crazy person will do. There were animal hides tacked to the walls, and steel traps hanging by chains that had either rust or dried blood still on them.

At one point, Wallace said around a mouthful of food, "This here is Gypsy Potash, and that lame boy out there taking care of the horses is her son, ain't that right, Gypsy?"

"You damn straight it's right. He come out of me with his foot all twisted up is why he's like that. Otherwise he'd be damn'd near a perfect speciman of manhoods."

Not that Albert nor me had asked or much cared.

We ate like thieves on the run with a posse on our heels. I kept an eye on the woman whose head was just an inch or two lower than the ceiling.

"This is mighty fair eating," I said, trying to be complimentary.

"Ain't it, though, for dog," she said.

That piece of meat I was just then chewing stuck in my gullet, halfway down but not sure it wanted to go the rest of the way to my belly. I glanced at Albert and he looked about as sick as I suddenly felt.

"She's just foolin' you," Alonzo said.

"Like hell I am," the woman said, then offered a high-pitched phlegmy laugh as she stirred whatever it was in a small kettle on the stove.

"Nah, you didn't," Wallace said.

"But come to think of it, I ain't seen Cooter about," Alonzo said. "Where is Cooter?"

"You mean this here is him we're eating?" Wallace said.

Then the woman laughed again until I thought she was going to choke on the plug of tobacco in her cheek.

"Nah, it ain't him," she said. "We et him last week."

"Well, I think I'm full up," Albert said, standing away from the table.

"Me too," I said.

She paid us no never mind as we went back outside into the night air.

"I think I'm going to puke," Albert said.

"I think I might join you," I said.

"Dog?" Albert said.

"I don't know, you ask me they all seem crazy enough that it is possible."

About then the Pallor brothers came outside and one of them relieved himself off the end of the porch while the other picked at his teeth with a thumbnail.

"Was she serious about that being dog we et?" Albert asked.

It was Wallace, I think, said, "Hell, who knows, she's as cracked as a cup."

"Yeah, hell, who knows, and who the hell cares," Alonzo said coming over from the end of the porch. "Least our bellies are full."

"You don't mind eating dog, if that is what it was?" Albert asked.

"Sonny, I've et a hell of a lot worse than dog, ain't I, Wallace?"

"We et a two-day old armadillo one time," Wallace said. "Down along the Rio Grande when we was chased by Apaches once and had to hide out for the day."

"That's right," Alonzo said, "but I don't reckon it tasted

164

worse than that gila monster we had for dessert."

Once more they broke into wild laughter.

I was still so queasy I forced myself to think of Jazzy just to get my mind off my belly, the good time we had back at the hotel, and stopped thinking just shy of when she . . .

"Well, who's going to go first," Alonzo said.

"Flip you for it, brother," Wallace said.

"First as to what?" I said.

"Oh, well, we didn't mean to leave you peckerwoods out. You're welcome to join in."

"What are you talking about?" Albert said.

"Well, we got to pay for those victuals someway," Wallace said. "So, whenever we stop here at the Gypsy's, we work it out in a carnal sense."

Albert looked at me as usual for the word's definition.

"Means she swaps that food for somebody having sexual relations with her," I said.

" 'Scuse me," Albert said and went running off.

"I think it's the dog that's made him ill," I said. "But, hey, you two go ahead and flip for it, I'm just fine staying out here."

"Doubt a little feller like yourself would do ol' Gypsy much good anyway," Alonzo said. They looked like a pair of ghosts standing out there under what was now a moonstruck landscape.

"You are a keen judge," I said.

Then they flipped a quarter and Alonzo won, or lost, depending on how a body thought of it, and back into the house he went.

Meanwhile Two Bits, the clubfooted son, returned from the barn, and watching him come along, that off foot seemed like it must weigh a hundred pounds the way he had to help lift it along.

"How is you peckerwoods?" he said, breathing hard, then flopped down on the edge of the porch.

It was Wallace's turn to make water off the end of the porch.

"Where's your little friend?" he asked.

"Albert? Oh, he's not feeling too well having et that dog meat stew."

"Yeah, my ma never was much of a cook, but somehow the fellers what stop by here don't seem to mind. Fact, they sometimes go back in for seconds and take a long time eating."

I fell silent trying not to think about it.

"Say, you want to see something I keep over in the barn yonder?"

"No, I think I'll sit right where I am, but thank you kindly, anyway." There was something about the whole bunch of them made me uneasy.

"Well, let me know if you change your mind," he said and went inside.

"That was smart of you to decline," Wallace said returning from the end of the porch and puffing on a cheroot. "That boy ain't all there."

"Is he crazy?" I said. "He seems all right but for that foot."

"He's more'n a little crazy," Wallace said, blowing a stream of smoke out of the side of his mouth. "He get you up in that barn, well, let's just say you'd never be the same."

I wasn't exactly sure what Wallace was getting at but I could kind of guess.

Albert returned about the time Alonzo came out of the house, his clothes askew and half unbuttoned and looking washed out.

"Next time we're through this way, let's just bypass this place," Wallace said flipping his cheroot out into the dark. "It ain't worth it, to eat dog on top of everything else."

So it *was* dog. And then it was my turn to head off and relieve my sickness but before I did I summoned Albert to come with me a little ways.

"Why are you acting so strange?" he said.

"Other'n, I just helped eat that woman's pet?" I said.

"Don't bring that subject up again with me. Ever, please."

"Word to the wise," I said trying to keep down what was wanting to come up. "Don't go into the barn with Two-Bits if he ask you."

"Why would he ask me?"

"Just don't, I got to go."

I hoped it was enough warning and surely it proved to be because when I got back Albert was still sitting there and not looking but poorly still.

"We going on tonight?" I said to Alonzo.

"We'll bunk out in the barn and head out first light," Alonzo said.

I lowered my voice to a near whisper and told him what Wallace had warned me about when Two Bits tried to lure me in there. He laughed sinisterly.

"That boy," he said shaking his head. "He's just a lonely little sucker that sees everything living as a possible companion if you know what I mean. We'll be all right in the barn there together. He comes around, just hit him with something and he'll leave you alone."

I could see the look of confusion on Albert's face and soon as the four of us went off to the barn. I glanced back once and saw Two Bits looking out of the window, his face like a jack-o'-lantern. Gave me the creeps.

Albert and me trailed behind the Pallor brothers, who seemed in a great hurry to get away from the house.

"Everything about this place, these people, gives me the willies," Albert said out of earshot.

"Me, as well," I said.

"I think we ought to just make a run for it after them Albinos are asleep."

"Are you forgetting our raison d'être?" I said. The study of

167

French and Latin was also a subject the nuns tried pounding into our heads. I only remembered certain things, phrases mostly.

"Our what?"

"The reason for what we're doing?" I said.

"Well, why didn't you just say that?"

"I just did."

"What's your point here, Ivory?"

"Listen, if I'm any judge of men, those two ghostly fellows are stone-cold killers, like they claim. And it just might be that is what we are in need of if we are to get Mrs. Pettymoney back. I don't reckon any place called the Robbers Roost is just somewhere we can stroll in and say hand her over and they will. I had a blood dream the other night."

"A blood dream?"

"You know what I'm talking about. Like the ones I had when we were chasing Rufus Buck and his gang."

"Oh, yeah."

"So, I reckon if there is bound to be blood, and what I seen in my dream there was plenty of it, we'll need those two."

"Ivory," he said in a weary voice. "I'm tired of chasing this damn One-eye Jack. I'd like to get this over with and then go on back to Last Whisky and see Ma and sleep in my bed and maybe start courting Sally Beth again if she ain't up and married somebody else. Then maybe just live a dang normal life for once. Wouldn't you?"

I understood fully what Albert was saying. I sort of missed the little Texas town myself, though there wasn't nothing there for me but my friend Albert, me being the only colored person there since Otero passed on.

"I feel the same way, Albert. But we gave that banker our word and you know as well as I do that a feller's word is his bond. We can't just slink on home like whipped dogs."

There came that word again and we both rushed over and retched up what little remained in our insides. I don't reckon I'd ever look at another dog again the same way.

We slept the night in the barn, but I made sure and kept one eye open in case the clubfoot came along. He didn't and the dawn light crept through the cracks in the barn in gray blades of light.

We all rustled out of our straw beds and stepped outside, me and Albert feeling much worse for the wear, whereas the Pallor boys headed toward the house.

"Where you headed?" I said. "I thought we were leaving out at first light."

"After we've et our breakfast," Alonzo said.

"Can't be traveling on an empty stomach, makes a man weak and when he's weakened, it can cut up to a second off your fast draw," Wallace said.

Albert and me stood and watched them go on into the witchy woman's house.

"What do you think?" I said to Albert.

"Not me," he said. "I'm still aching in my ribs from throwing up last evening."

"Maybe she's serving cat this morning," I said.

"That's not even funny," Albert said.

We went to the corral and put ropes around our horses and led them out and started in saddling them.

"Did that clubfoot come around last night?" Albert asked over the back of his saddle as he was tightening the cinch.

"Not that I know of," I said.

"You really think it's going to turn into a bloody fight when we get to Robbers Roost?"

"Well, if it does, I just hope none of the blood is ours or that of Mrs. Pettymoney," I said.

We got our mounts saddled and waited for the Pallors and

after a time they came out of the house and over to the corral.

"How was breakfast?" Albert said.

"Fine," Alonzo said.

"Mush with biscuits and honey," said Wallace.

"Real good tasting," said Alonzo.

Albert and me exchanged looks.

"Any left?" I said.

"Some," Wallace said.

"You best run in there and eat, we're wasting time standing around here."

"What do you think?" I asked Albert.

"I think mush and biscuits and honey sounds pretty sweet."

So off we went and inside at the table was the witchy woman and Two Bits swiping up the leavings on their plates.

"Help yourselves," the witchy woman said.

We did and ate fast and got back out to the corral just as the Pallors were mounting up.

We set off on the west road but had not gone far when Wallace opined: "You know, now that I think about it, I'm wondering if that really was mush or something else we et?"

"I was thinking the same thing," Alonzo said.

"Well what could it have been do you think?" said Wallace.

Alonzo shook his head dramatically.

"Could have been some sort of brains she mashed up," he said.

"Well, if it was, them brains was mighty tasty," Wallace said.

Albert started to turn pale, his face screwed up at the thought we'd possibly et mashed-up brains.

"They're just stirring your beans," I told Albert. "I've et a lot of mush and that wasn't any brains. That was cornmeal made with good cow's milk."

He looked somewhat relieved. I wasn't at all sure myself but I wished it so and so it was.

After we rode on farther with the sun burning off the morning fog and the day growing warmer, I asked Alonzo how much farther did he reckon it was until we reached the Robbers Roost.

He looked skyward as if the answer was up there in the blue, then said, "Oh, I guess twenty miles, something like that."

I didn't know how he knew that; there was nothing outstanding to mark the passage by such as a rock-cairn broken tree.

"Well, what do you imagine will happen when we do get there?" Albert said.

For a time neither brother answered and then Wallace spoke up.

"The plan is to get your woman back," he said. "And to do that, if it is as you say and she is in the hands of One-eye Texas Jack Crowfoot, of whom I have intimate knowledge, I reckon the killing will commence."

"It must," said Alonzo, "and when it does commence, me and Wallace here will be the ones to commence it."

"Always shoot first, our daddy told us."

"And ask your questions later," Alonzo confirmed.

"We'd prefer getting her back with as little slaughter as possible," Albert said.

"Oh, well, then you just go on in there, sonny, and tell them that's what you'd like and I'm sure they'll oblige," Alonzo said with a snicker.

"You boys ever been in a gunfight?" Wallace said.

"Ever killed anyone?" Alonzo said.

"Not exactly," I said.

This was when they both started laughing again.

"Not exactly!"

"But we've seen men killed," Albert said.

They laughed all the harder.

"If you two sisters want to wait outside somewhere while me and Wallace go in and take care of business and bring you the lady," Alonzo said, "it'll cost you the entire reward."

"But what if . . ." Albert seemed lost in his question as if the words he was about to speak were like butterflies and just flew off somewhere.

"You don't have to worry about Albert and me," I said. "We'll hold our own and do whatever it takes."

"Our word is our bond, ain't that so, Ivory?" Albert confirmed, though he had a bit of a quaver in his voice.

"It is," I said, trying to keep the quaver out of my own voice.

By midday, the sun was desperately hot and the boys said that they had to get in the shade somewhere.

" 'Cause we're Albinos and the sun is hard on us," Alonzo said as we eased into a copse of cottonwoods whose limbs reminded me of mottled bone.

We loosened the cinches on our mounts and gratefully there was a running creek close at hand and me and Albert walked the horses off to let them drink.

"You know what I think?" Albert said, out of earshot of the Pallors.

"What's that?" I said.

"I think we're going to be killed, either by One-eye and his gang, or by them," he said, glancing over his shoulder to where the boys lay stretched out in the deep shade.

Albert looked at me waiting for an answer.

"You afraid of death?" he said.

"No, but I just as soon not be there when it happens," I replied.

He found no humor in my answer and to tell the truth, I'm not sure I did, either.

"What do you think happens to a body when we die?" he asked.

"Well, according to my friend, Sister Mary Virgin, we go and meet our maker and if he determines we've lived a righteous life, we get into heaven and if not, we are cast into a lake of fire."

Albert mused on this for a time.

"I think I'd not like to die before I, well, you know, like what you and Jazzy did back at the hotel."

"Trust me, you don't want to with her being married and all."

"No, I don't mean with *her*, I mean what the two of you did."

"So you never did then?"

He blushed, said, "Just come close with Geneva is all."

"I'll tell you what," I said. "We make it out alive and get our share of the reward money, first thing we're going to do is visit a house of ill repute and rent you the prettiest gal in the place."

"No, Ivory, I want it to be with Sally Beth, my sweetheart back in Last Whisky. I want it to be special."

"Well, maybe you should consider practicing first," I said. "I'm sure you pay the right girl she'll teach you what you need to know whenever you get around to being with your sweetheart."

Between the prospects of getting dead and still being a virgin, Albert looked mighty conflicted.

CHAPTER 12

The Pallors, having helped cool themselves down by dipping their neckerchiefs in the stream and laying them across their foreheads, waited until the sun lowered off into the west before we again climbed back on our horses. Just more time for me and Albert to get more nervous about the coming bloodletting by the way the Albinos continued talking about the variety and type of men who sought refuge in the Robbers Roost.

"Why, every blackguard, cutthroat, backshooter, and low skunk on two legs has gathered there at one time or another," Alonzo said.

"It's so bad a place, you couldn't pay a lawman to go in there," Wallace said.

"And if you could, which you can't, that'd be the last anyone ever saw of him," Alonzo said. "Even the women in there are bad."

"Real bad," Alonzo confirmed.

"It's truly a bad place," said Wallace.

"The worst," said Alonzo.

"I think you made your point," said Albert. "That it is a bad place and the folks in it are bad."

"Why, whatever give you that idea, sonny?" Wallace said.

This set them to laughing again.

"Even the horses is bad," Wallace said.

"And so is the dogs," Alonzo said.

I was starting to get a headache and wondered if anyone had

174

ever told those Albinos how much they could fray a body's nerves with their getting carried away.

We were riding directly into the setting sun, causing us to squint and pull the brims of our hats low over our eyes. But the Pallors produced glasses with smoked lenses in them so that they looked even more odd. I'd never seen such glasses before but it seemed to me I'd read somewhere that Wild Bill had himself a pair on account of his having eye problems later on in life. Of course, that could have been a rumor started by the writer of that particular dime book. It wouldn't be the first time some writer had stretched the truth. I never could verify later on as I got older whether or not the story was actually true, but having seen the Albinos wearing those special glasses, I tended to believe that perhaps it was so.

Just about the time all the good sun had settled in off beyond the hills and left the sky the color of brass all around and some into shadows, we saw up ahead and off to our right a smattering of what at first looked like lightning bugs.

"There it is," Wallace said.

"Robbers Roost," Alonzo confirmed.

I suddenly felt the need to relieve myself.

"I got to stop," I said.

"What for?" Alonzo wanted to know.

"To make water."

"Make water?" Wallace said.

"How do you make water?"

"Pee," I said.

"Well, why didn't you say that?" Alonzo said.

"On account of I was raised in an orphanage around decent womenfolk and that's how I was taught to talk about it."

"Well, Wallace, you got to make water too?" Alonzo sniggered.

"I do if you do," Wallace sniggered back.

The four of us dismounted and stood facing in four different directions so as not to shame ourselves by looking at the other or being looked at.

"Hey, Nig," Wallace shouted over his shoulder.

"What?" I said over my own shoulder.

"What'd you call it around them decent women when you had to shit?"

"Number two," I said.

"Number two," Alonzo sniggered some more.

I heard them giggling like girls and then I heard Albert give a snort too.

"Don't encourage them," I said.

"I ain't, Ivory," he said, then snorted again.

After we finished we got back on our horses and Wallace said, "Is there anything else you got to make, like a pie or something, or should we just go on in and commence the slaughter?"

"I'm good," I said, "you good too, Albert?"

"I'm good too."

"No," I said to the man killers. "Don't seem like we have to make nothing else."

I couldn't tell rightly but I bet those Albinos were grinning like jack-o'-lanterns.

We mounted up to make the final push toward our destination and already we could hear the loud voices and fires being lit. None of it offered comfort to Albert and me.

Perhaps this would be the time to talk about our encounter with the murderous Rufus Buck when we finally tracked him to a house of ill repute and braced him as he took a bubble bath with one of the denizens of that establishment. And, though we had every intent of doing what might need doing, such as filling the dirty cuss full of our lead, it wasn't Albert or me who shot Rufus dead as a stone. The actual shooter was a fellow called himself Preacher who vowed he loved the Lord as much as he loved naked women and good liquor. It can honestly be said about Preacher that while he wasn't perfect, his heart was always in the right place, just as it was that day, or else Albert and me would be long moldering in our graves and not heading into outlaws' refuge with a couple of very white gunslingers.

Lord, I prayed (even though I wasn't one hundred percent sure of what I'd been taught at the orphanage about the power of prayer), *don't let Albert and me get killed, 'cause he sure would like to see his ma again and I'd like to . . . well, I'd like to just keep on living. As far as those Albinos, well, I've got no say in the matter, but if they are to give up the ghost, so to speak, and I don't mean to be making a joke about it, please let it be after they drill One-eye Texas Jack Crowfoot through the brisket. And also, let us rescue poor Mrs. Pettymoney, for every bride should get a chance to enjoy her wedding night, at least once. Well, Lord, maybe I shouldn't get into that part of it. But you know what I mean. Amen.*

Robbers Roost, proved to be a collection of scabrous shanties that clung to the side of a hill mostly, like scabs on a diseased man's body. They looked downright urchin and I should know what urchin looks like. I got the feeling it was like demons were watching us from those shanties. Mangy dogs, some of which lay there in the middle of the road, pricked their ears and barked diseased barks that sounded like the coughing of old men, and dirty-faced children stood and stared after us as if we were the Second Coming, which we were most certainly the farthest thing from.

"How are we going to know which one of these places is One-eye's?" Albert asked Wallace, having ridden up alongside him.

"We'll go on down to the saloon. If he's here, we'll find out."

"We'll sure find out," confirmed Alonzo.

Albert dropped back alongside of me.

"Why is it all the really bad men seek their comfort in saloons, do you think?" he said.

"Guess it's where they do their drinking," I said. "Far as I know you can't buy whiskey and wanton women in church." Albert gave me a sour look.

What with the bloodshot eye of the sun's last and eyes watching us from the shanties, it was like we were riding into a frightful dream. The entire place was a lot larger and more desperate looking than I had imagined. I didn't realize so many of the criminal element existed all in one place. But then I reasoned, what better place for them than in the same place.

Here and there loud conversations could be heard coming from some of the shanties, arguing mostly, babies squalling, dogs barking, kids shouting, maniacs cussing.

But some of the shanties appeared as if unlived in, their residents perhaps away or dead, though the one thing I didn't spot was a graveyard, which gave me the smallest comfort.

At last, we came to a long-slung log building booming with more yelps and curses and laughter and the high-pitched cries of females. There were perhaps two dozen saddle horses tied up out front, a few wagons as well, along with several men lazing about with crock jugs hooked on forefingers.

"This is it," Wallace said.

"If your man is in Robbers Roost, we'll most likely learn of him here," Wallace said.

"And if we do, we'll kill him."

"After we learn where Mrs. Pettymoney is," I reminded.

"Tittey," Alonzo said and grinned.

We reined in and dismounted

"How are we going to do this?" Albert said.

"What do you mean?" Wallace said.

"I mean, should me and Ivory go in back while you and Alonzo take the front, or the other way around?"

I thought it was a valid tactical point.

Alonzo looked at Albert as if he was daft—Albert, I mean, not Alonzo—and said, "Don't give a rat's hinny what you two do, but me and Wallace is just going to go in there and if we see One-eye, we're going to kill him. Then you can wire for the reward and we'll be on our way."

"But not before we find out what he did with Mrs. Pettymoney," I said once more, and two pairs of red eyes landed on me like the measles.

"You want him dead or not?"

"Yes," I said. "But it will do us little good unless we can get her. Her husband is paying the reward for her return, not One-eye's death."

"What good would that do him otherwise?" Albert concluded.

Both of the Pallor brothers shook their heads as if to tell us we were fools.

"Okay, we won't kill him until he tells us where he's keeping the woman," Wallace said. "We'll just shoot him some till he talks."

"And then we'll kill him," Alonzo said.

"Fair enough," I said, for their manly talk had me fired up.

"Maybe save Ivory and me some to shoot at too," Albert said. He was also fired up. It's a funny thing about vengeance, you want it against your better judgment; that's how we were feeling just then, Albert and me. I wanted to rescue Mrs. Pettymoney and I wanted to assure we'd done our duty in getting Gus a real good burying and perhaps some vengeance on his killer. It seems only natural a friend would think in those terms.

When Albert said that about him and me getting in our licks on One-eye Jack, the Pallors showed their pearly teeth in a double grin.

"Well, all right then, we'll all go in and look for this bride stealer," Alonzo said.

"First one spots him—if'n it's you two—come get Alonzo

and me, let us hash his bacon to get him to talk. We know how to do it."

"Agreed," I said.

Inside, what with the air thick with cigar smoke and the sweating mass of humanity, made it hard to distinguish any one individual even though there were lighted lamps hanging from the rafters overhead.

"Let's stick close, Albert," I said as the Pallors went off in one direction and me and Albert in the other.

The first thing I laid eyes on I could make out was a good-sized woman standing on a table with the top of her dress pulled down shaking her bosoms at a group of gathered men who were braying like a pack of mules, and, in turn, she was braying back. I took note that every man jack of those around the table were well-armed, with hip holsters that flowered pistol grips.

I turned around to point out the brazen woman to Albert but he was gone.

"Albert?" I called but my voice was lost in all that noise like a whisper in a storm.

"Albert," I shouted and someone slapped me on the back and I turned to see who it was had taken such liberty and it was an overly large man with a bloated face the color of a ripe apple.

"Hey there, Nig," he shouted, then wobbled away and I darn near shot him until I saw he was just being friendly in the way drunks are sometimes friendly.

I turned about trying to spot Albert and caught a glimpse of him up on a catwalk overhead that went past several closed curtains. He was struggling to loose himself from a woman who was even bigger than the one atop the table doing her shimmy to get the boys to bidding for her as I realized she was being auctioned off by a man in a black silk hat who held a quart bottle of whiskey in one hand and a lit cigar in the other.

I called and waved to Albert, even as I was walled off by men as large as steers. But Albert held his own and soon freed himself from her grasp and came flying down a set of stairs at the back wall and worked his way to where I stood.

"She tried to kidnap me," he shouted in my ear. "Said she wanted to take me home and marry me."

"What'd you tell her?"

"I told her I was already married."

"Good answer," I said.

He shook his head.

"I couldn't tell if you were trying to get free of her or she of you," I joked.

"Well, what do you think, Ivory? She told me she didn't care if I was married or diseased or nothing long as I had a buck to give her." He shook his head in dismay.

"Well, that just ain't right of her," I said. "Fact, it is just plain wrong. I'm glad you got loose of that gal. Who knows where you'd have ended up if you hadn't."

"Boy, don't I know it? If my ma ever heard I was in a place like this with these sort of ladies, she'd skin me good," he said, his eyes frightful.

"You could call them a lot of things, Albert, but I don't think ladies is one of them."

Albert looked a bit frightful but still resolute.

"Say, did you spot those Pallor brothers from up there?"

"It was hard to spot much of anything, rassling as I was. Plus, there is so many galoots crowded in here, I think we'll have to search for 'em."

"Let's go see can we find them whilst still keeping an eye out for Texas Jack," I said.

"Well, what if we see One-eye first?"

"Let's hope we find them Albinos first."

Just then gunfire shattered through the room.

Bang! Bang! Bang! Bang!

Screams. Lots of screams, and some cussing too as men ran into each other trying to make the door and go out the windows and women sounded like they were being ravaged by savages.

But then it grew quiet for a time, Albert and me lying flat on the floor like some others had as well. Fact, if we could have crawled under the floorboards, I think we would have. I saw one man down on his belly holding a mug of beer as if it was his inheritance. Even the big gal that had been atop the table being auctioned off was down on the floor lying under the man who'd been auctioning her.

Then someone shouted: "Goddamn, you just killed them freaks!"

"What the hell are them creatures, anyway?" somebody else shouted.

"Never seen nothing like 'em," yet another voice called out.

"Somebody bleached all the color out of 'em," still another voice added.

"Oh, oh," Albert whispered. "I do believe maybe they are talking about the Pallor boys."

"Can't be," I whispered back.

"Who else does it sound like?" Albert whispered back to me once more.

Then folks started moving around talking more and more, all of them pushing to the far end of the saloon where the gunfire had come from as if in a rush to see what it was those fellows were talking about.

"Let's proceed easy," I said to Albert as we got up off that filthy floor and brushed away what we could that had gotten onto our clothes.

We worked our way through the crowd of people who were jabbering to one another like folks waiting to get inside a circus tent to see an oddity. And Albert and me caught just a glimpse of the Pallor brothers stretched out on the floor looking even whiter and more ghostly than they had been in life; bloodless would be the apt word to describe them. A creeping puddle of what had once flowed through their veins, as red as any other kind of blood, spread out from their bodies. Wallace lay facedown and Alonzo faceup, his red eyes open and staring, I suppose, at that place the newly dead see as their final destination.

Standing above them was one One-eye Texas Jack Crowfoot, smoke leaking from the guns in his hands like Satan's own breath. Around him stood two or three others I assumed were part of his gang, their guns also smoking, the barrels probably hot to the touch.

I noticed, too, that Alonzo had a newly formed third eye in the center of his forehead nearly the same redness of his regular eye with a trickle of blood oozing forth, giving him the queer look of a man with three red eyes and not a single one to see with.

I whispered to Albert to go out and get the now defunct Pallors' horses and put them with ours and keep to the edge of the copse of woods that ringed the settlement and I'd come find him in a bit.

"Why don't you come with me?" he said out of the side of his mouth.

"I just want to try and come up with a plan while you be ready to make our escape."

So, he slipped away while I watched the men gathered around the dead brothers.

Wallace had several bloody spots in his back as well as half his skull blown away and it made me think about Gus, how he had met a similar fate. That undertaker had been right about One-eye being an assassin by shooting out brains.

Somebody said "the word is 'Albinos,' that's what they are," and somebody else said, "I heard of 'em." And somebody else

183

said, "I seen the likes of one in a circus one time in Cheyenne, called the fellow a White Nigger, said he was from Borneo or someplace like that, called him a freak of nature and that he was the only known one in the entire world and charged two bits a head to look at him."

Somebody else piped up and said: "Well, it's obvious he warn't the only one in the world since they is two lying right there. I'd say you got took, Sandy."

One-eye Texas Jack Crowfoot, but not Mrs. Pettymoney, was among the lot, which told me she was either dead, sheltered somewhere, or sold. But maybe, I thought hopefully, she was being kept in one of the shanties we'd rode past on the way in.

One-eye was staring down at the corpses of the Pallors with that lone glaring eye full of vexation, his mouth grim, as he reloaded his hulls in order to shoot them—*Bang!*—deader than they already were and with each extra slug he fired into them, the other boys in the room cheered him on: "That's right, Jack, let 'em have it!"

Bang!

"Don't trust them freaks, Jack, they're liable to come back to life."

Bang!

"I don't know why these birds was trying to assassinate me," Jack declared after emptying his gun into the poor boys, "but this is what you get when you come after Texas Jack Crowfoot!" I noted how he left out that One-eye part of his moniker. Most likely a point of vanity. But it wasn't just the eye patch, or the long scar on his face, or nothing else, the man was plain ugly the way some of nature's creatures are ugly: the turkey buzzard and suck toad and catfish.

Once more he reloaded and once more took aim.

Bang! Bang! Bang! his revolvers announced, and the onlookers jumped a little each time.

184

When he was satisfied he'd killed the Albinos enough, he barked an order: "Take these—whatever the hell you called them—outside and hang 'em up in the hanging tree, for they will provide good target practice for anyone wants to pay me a dollar. Now serve up that goddamn liquor, dad, for I'm all athirst!"

It was about then that the formerly naked sporting gal shoved through and pushed up against One-eye and cuddled and cooed as he put an arm around her thick waist.

"Sadie, how's about we take a bottle upstairs, for my loins are all aflame."

A few men dragged the Pallor brothers out by their heels, leaving a swath of blood across the floor like a bad paint job while the others rushed the bar and ordered drinks.

It was just at that point my gaze noticed a familiar face sitting over in one corner with a winsome wench riding his lap, the two of them paying attention to no one else but each other.

Preacher.

The sight of him both lifted and dashed my spirits. I hadn't seen him since he drilled Rufus Buck that day in the bathtub, sinking him like a stone while the harlot Rufus was dallying with ran screaming out of the room like it was she Preacher had murdered.

I had to look twice to make sure. Preacher had grown gaunt with a dark scraggly beard. He seemed more shopworn than last I'd seen him, which was when he'd saved the lives of Albert and me by dousing out the lights of the notorious killer Rufus Buck.

Gus Monroe, the gunfighter extraordinaire, and now passed from this mortal coil and me and Albert's reason for being here, was the first gunfighter we'd gotten to help us. The problem, though we had not known it at the time, was that Gus had gone beyond his prime—something he himself did not know until the time for action presented itself. Too late, we all learned Ol' Gus no longer had the sand, or the skills, to take on the youth and deadly skills of Rufus Buck. Only the man who hauls the load knows for certain if the load has become too heavy to haul. In fact, had Gus not recognized his limitations before we found Rufus, a vicious little killer half Gus's age, Rufus would have most likely put Gus in his grave before now.

Rufus and his gang were the meanest homicidal fools in all the West at the time when they were on the rage, raping and murdering innocent folks for the thrill of it. Thankfully, their killing reign hadn't lasted that long due to Albert and me's thirst for revenge over Albert's pa's killing. Luckily, we met Preacher, who bore no one any ill will, a man of such a noble and peaceful heart he gave us a sense of calm and serenity. But Preacher riled was no man to toy with and he had no problem drilling you if you needed the drilling.

I'd say of all the people I've ever know, Preacher was the most enigmatic (another word supplied to me by Mr. Webster's book) of the lot. If I had to sum Preacher up, he was a devout, whore-mongering, praying, whiskey-drinking fool who had probably killed as many men as he'd saved in service of the Lord. Though I suppose that fact could be arguable, and the exact number unknown. Let's just say it was some of this and some of that when it came down to saving and killing. Wherever Preacher went, trouble seemed to follow, or in many cases, waiting on him like an irate husband, which made me think of Jazzy right off.

So, in a way, I was not completely surprised to see Preacher there in that scurrilous den of iniquity, but in another way, I was disappointed to see he had not changed old habits. If anything, he looked aged a good bit, maybe because of the drinking and womanizing and so forth.

I slunk out the door and went where I'd told Albert to hold the horses.

"Well?" Albert said.

"The Pallor brothers are being strung up in that big cotton-wood out front of the saloon and in no more position to help us, Albert," I said.

"Why are they being strung up, I thought they were already dead," Albert said.

"For target practice," I said.

"Here we go again," Albert groaned.

"Wait," I said. "In a way it is a good news, bad news thing."

"How so, Ivory?"

"Well, the good news is, we save half the reward money we were going to pay those Albinos, and the bad news is pretty obvious."

"I heard more gunfire, after you left," Albert said. "I was about to come over there for fear you'd gotten into trouble."

"No, Texas Jack was just killing those Pallor brothers again and again before he had them strung up. Out of pure hatred," I said.

"You said not having to split the reward money with the Pal-lors was the good news," Albert said. "Is there any other good news?"

"We might just have an ace in the hole," I said.

"Did you go to gunfighting school since I seen you last?" he said. I suppose to be meant as a joke. Albert never was much good at joke telling.

"Better than that," I said. "There is a very old and very dear friend of ours inside."

Albert looked at me dully.

"Didn't know we had any friends that weren't dead," he said.

"Preacher," I said.

"Preacher? *A* preacher, or do you mean the one called

187

Preacher who helped us out with Rufus Buck?"

"The latter," I said.

Albert suddenly looked all around.

"What are you looking for?" I said.

"The ladder. You said there was a ladder."

"No, the *latter*," I said pronouncing it more clearly. Sometimes I talk too fast and my words don't come out precisely, and I'm working on that.

"Oh, you mean Rufus's slayer," he said.

"Indeed, I do."

Suddenly the sky burst open and let loose with a downpour of rain so hard and furious I thought Albert and me might have to swim our way out of the encampment. And Mrs. Pettymoney, if we could ever locate her, might have to swim too. Albert opined that maybe the Lord intended on wiping out the whole nest of miscreants there in Robbers Roost, and us along with it. It rained so hard and loudly we could barely hear ourselves shouting above the deluge.

"It happened to Noah," Albert shouted.

"We ain't him," I shouted back.

"I know we ain't, but I don't reckon he knew he was him until it happened," Albert said.

"Why would God want to drown you and me along with the likes of the rest of 'em inside what done the murdering?" I yelled.

"I reckon like in old Noah's time, he just got fed up and wants to start over again."

I could but shake my head at Albert's take on matters, but I recalled Sister Mary Virgin saying much the same thing when she talked about the great flood. I looked skyward and the rain almost punched my eyeballs out. I wished I'd learned how to swim.

We tied off the horses and ran back inside the saloon just to keep from drowning, it being the only dry place we could think of, though once inside, we saw the roof had sprung several leaks, which nobody seemed to pay much attention to.

Preacher was still sitting there toying with the woman on his lap and she toying with him such that it made me a bit jealous that the only woman who had toyed with me had then confessed to being married, a point of fact that would not in the least have disturbed Preacher—or at least it would not have in the past.

"There he sits yonder," I said to Albert.

"Blamed if it ain't him," Albert said. "He's already killed one man for us. You reckon he'd kill another?"

"I don't see why he wouldn't," I said

"He looks a bit run-down since we seen him last, Ivory?"

"True, but maybe his trigger finger ain't worn down," I said.

Meanwhile, on account of the rain, even more people had clamored inside the saloon than was there before. The sporting gals were in their element and doing a brisk business as well as the beer jockeys. The blood of the Albinos still lay in double long swaths from where they were gunned down all the way to the door and out. By some strange coincidence, the rain leaking down had missed their mark when it came to the blood.

"Maybe paying Preacher to be on our side wouldn't be a bad idea," I said.

"It would be a very good idea," Albert agreed.

Now that the day's entertainment of killing was over, some of the galoots at the bar started peering around at Albert and me, but mostly at me, and I could hear such words as "Nig" and "Darkie" being spoken.

I began to think that maybe they'd already grown bored with nothing to do but drink and cuss and wait their turn with one of the sporting girls to be available, that maybe they'd like some more murderous entertainment.

"I'm thinking maybe I should go on back to where we left

the horses," I said to Albert. "I'm starting to feel like the only hog at a barbecue."

Albert cast me a doubtful eye.

"You go on soon as you can work your way over to Preacher and give him the word I'm outside and we'd like to talk to him about something most important, something that had good money attached to it."

"Why don't we do it together, Ivory?"

I told him he would draw less attention than I, a black child carrying a pistol, would and besides somebody had to stand watch with the horses and I'd had my fill of the place anyway, the slaughter, and all and fat ladies asking me to buy them a drink. Then he noticed how some of those men at the bar was looking at me too.

"All right," he said. "You go on and I'll see can I talk Preacher into coming out with me and meeting you where we got the horses."

I was already going through the door by the time he said "horses" and back out in the downpour and happy to be getting soaked to the bones again. It felt a lot better than a fusillade (read that in a DeWitt's dime books and looked it up in the dictionary) of lead.

As I splashed toward where we'd tied the horses, I recalled the many times Otero, my master teacher of building coffins and a crazy old coot, but kind, as well, told me how often he'd been shot. Thirteen times, he said, and showed me the puckered flesh where bullets had gone in or come out.

"*Ay, caramba!*" he would say, sipping a bottle of mescal, something he always kept close, like a lover. "It hurts like hell, sometimes, and sometimes ju done even feel it."

I told him he was lucky in spite of the number thirteen.

"Jes," he said. "Many time they try to kill me, but many time they don't, eh."

I liked the crazy old man, for he was full of humor and (this one I had to look up in the dictionary to find the word I wanted to most accurately describe him as) *pathos*. Yes, that was Otero—either laughing or near crying when he spoke of the old days and filling me with pity for him when he got down like that.

Funny the things you think about at the oddest times. Maybe it was the rain, for I found him dead on a day like this, raining hard when it hardly ever rained in that part of Texas. I'd gone into the shed where we built the coffins. I say "we" but it was mostly me doing the measuring, sawing, planing, and hammering, and Otero watching and remembering what it had been like when he was a young bandito being chased by the Federales, lawmen, angry husbands, and crazy women.

But on that morning, he was neither drinking nor dreaming, but lying silent on the ground like he'd simply lain down and gone to sleep. I shook him and tried to wake him, but there was no waking of the dead and finally I just squatted down on my heels and wept for a long time, and when the rain at last stopped, I got up and built him the finest coffin I could.

As I waited under the cottonwoods that gave little to no shelter from the rain, one yellow cur trotted over to where I stood and sniffed my ankles.

"Get," I said.

It looked up at me with golden curious eyes.

"Ain't you got nothing better to do than sniff me?" I said. "Get now."

But instead it stood there next to me staring off at something and when I looked that direction I saw what the dog was looking at. The bodies of the Pallor brothers hanging upside down from the mottled bone limb of a cottonwood tree so big it looked like it had been there since biblical times. Their arms and hands seemed to be reaching for the cratered puddles beneath them they couldn't quite touch, nor would they until someone cut them down and buried them. It was a ghastly sight.

I was distracted momentarily by a fellow who came to the door of the saloon and pitched out a bucket of pinkish water no doubt from mopping up the blood inside.

"You see that?" I said to the dog. It whimpered as if to say, Yes, I seen it.

"What's your name mongrel?"

Again it looked up at me and I at it but it only whimpered and I told it I didn't understand no kind of dog talk and it ought to just save its breath and go on to wherever it come from and at least get dry and maybe beg a scrap of something. Finally, it trotted over to where those dead Albinos hung and raised up on its hind legs and licked their bloody fingertips, then looked back up to me and I told it I didn't have no truck with blood-licking dogs and it trotted off and went on around one of the buildings.

Dogs, I thought, who could account for them?

Pretty soon I saw Albert coming out of the whiskey den's door and trotting straight over to where I stood and looked back only once.

"Well?" I said.

"Preacher was glad to see me and learn we were yet living and breathing and not killed. Said he had often prayed for our safety after the Rufus Buck affair," Albert said.

He looked most pleased and I was, too, to hear Preacher hadn't forgotten us.

"That's what he called it?" I said. "The Rufus Buck affair?"

I could just see a new dime book with that title and starring Albert and me and a duded-up Preacher on the cover, guns blazing, the three of us a menace to any bad men.

"He wanted to know about you," Albert said. "I told him you were out here holding horses and he sort of laughed and said,

'What's that dang rock head doing standing out in the rain holding horses for?' and I told him, 'For a little while' and he got a laugh out of that. But then I said if he could see his way clear, maybe he could come on out and meet with us because I didn't really want to talk in front of that woman he had sitting on his lap. She looked untrustworthy, Ivory, and gave me a look like she wanted to eat me alive."

"I don't know what it is about you, Albert, that gets all the wrong kind of females favoring you, but they sure enough do. What'd Preacher say to your proposal?"

"He said soon as he could he would, but that he had a little something more to take care of—some business. But he said also he had a big Sibley tent set up at the back of these trees and we could wait there for him, if we liked, or, we could just keep standing out in this rain if we hadn't learned anything since that last time we'd seen him."

"Well, what'll you think, Albert, wait here or go wait in the tent outta this rain?" I said.

"I think . . ." It took him a whole second to see I was stirring his beans.

"Well, dang you, Ivory."

So, we went on through the small copse of trees and saw the big Sibley pitched and we tied off the horses to a rope remuda Preacher had strung there with a pair of his own horses, then got inside where it was nice and dry. And no sooner had we ducked inside, then it stopped raining and it was hot again in no time flat, maybe even hotter, and certainly steamier.

We found a kerosene lantern hanging from a hook screwed into the center pole and a box of matches and fired the wick and suddenly the inner gloom was lifted. We stripped out of our duds and stepped back out and wrung as much water out of them as we could and poured the water out of our boots and hung our clothes off the guy ropes to let them dry.

"I wonder who Preacher stole this tent off of?" Albert said.

"Maybe he bought it, or won it in a poker game?" I said.

"Or maybe some daughter of darkness gave it to him."

"Well, Preacher is the sort that makes foolish women want to do things for him. He's got that way about him."

There was a cot with blankets on it and we wrapped up in those nice wool blankets and Albert said as we sat around on the floor of grass that he felt like we was Indians way out on the plains waiting to go buffalo hunting.

"Or have our squaws fix us some buffalo stew and sew us new moccasins," I said.

"I'd have me two or three wives," Albert said "and plenty of horses, not just one. And I'd be a brave warrior who collected many scalps from my enemies."

"Well, you got three horses already," I said. "Yours and the Pallor brothers."

He grimaced and said, "I don't feel right taking their horses, do you, Ivory?"

"I don't feel wrong about it," I said. "If we didn't take them those cutthroats and brigands around here surely would. I wonder who got their guns and boots?"

"Wonder what Preacher is doing with this bunch?" Albert said. "It ain't like him to be hanging about with low characters. I mean, I don't think it is."

"Maybe he lost Jesus and found the devil," I said.

"Still . . ."

"Preacher is probably doing what he's always doing, getting along to get along," I said. "You know Preacher, he'd rather drink and make love to a pretty gal, or an ugly one for that matter, than do desperate things. At least I hope he hasn't thrown in with One-eye Jack and his ilk."

The stuffy air inside the tent left us feeling sleepy the way such conditions will do.

"You think she's here, Mrs. Pettymoney?" Albert said as we stretched out.

"I'm hoping she is and not dead or sold off to Comancheros to be taken across the border. Worse would be to be too ruined by that kidnapper and murderer."

"You think she would be, ruined, I mean?" Albert said.

"Yes, Albert, I think Texas Jack would have taken every advantage of her he could. He doesn't strike me as a man who would hold back any of his ruinous desires, especially after I saw how he drilled those poor Pallor boys over and over even after they were already dead. He is a man who lacks moral fiber."

"A no-good low dog," Albert said.

"Black-hearted."

"Evil itself."

"The devil's own."

Then we ran out of bad things to say about One-eye, though I'm sure there were a lot more things we could have said.

For a moment Albert didn't say anything but I knew what he was thinking: About how such an innocent woman would or could deal with the depravities of a scoundrel like Texas Jack and his gang. For surely if Jack got his way with her, it was possible his gang had too, though such thoughts sickened me.

"If she's here and alive," I said, "I reckon it's better no matter what she might of had to suffer, than be dead or traded off and sold across the border where she'd never be found."

I didn't fully believe such things, for if I was Mrs. Pettymoney and sorely violated as such, I'd just as soon be dead. But I wanted Albert to believe anything was better than death for her, for he was a boy of greater sensitivities than myself, having been taught good life's lessons, passed on to him by his ma, who was for my money, a saint of a woman.

The next I knew I was being shaken awake and smelling

whiskey breath and perfume coming off Preacher, who was bent over waggling my foot.

"Well, about the last souls on earth I ever expected to see again were the two of you, especially in this camp," he said sliding up one of two camp chairs and plopping in it, then stretching out his legs, his knee-length boots mud slathered.

"We're just as surprised to see you here, Preacher," I said.

He waved a hand, his eyes partly glazed over from the effects of drink and damsels, I suppose it was. More and more lately, as I read the dime novels, I've come to think of things in flowery terms like how the writers had wrote them, and even considered the possibility of Albert and me writing our own books; I guess this is sort of the beginning of my literary career if'n I ain't killed here in this awful place.

"The Lord sends his messengers into not the places that don't need them, but the ones that do, such as here in Robbers Roost," Preacher said.

"Ones with whiskey and women and gambling and such?" Albert said. I couldn't tell if he was being naïve or stirring Preacher's beans.

"Exactly, my young friend," Preacher said.

"And are you getting the word across?" Albert asked.

"Doing my damnedest." Preacher smiled.

Albert and me explained the whole thing, about Gus being murdered and Mrs. Pettymoney's kidnapping, the Pallor brothers, and so on, including the reward that Mr. Pettymoney had put up and the promise to see that Gus got a decent funeral.

"Well, those are some fine reasonings," Preacher declared, taking a silver flask from inside his coat and extending it to us, which we declined. He eyed the flask appreciatively as if it were a new harlot he'd just been introduced to.

"It's a gift from an old lady friend," he said; he put it to his mouth and drank, then smiled. "Sweet nectar of life, boys. You

don't know what you're missing. But then, it's too early for you
boyos to start down the path of no redemption. I ought to know,
I'm almost at the end of it myself."

He drank some more, then held the flask away.

"Say, you boyos have grown a lick since last I seen you, shot
up like weeds you have." It sort of made us feel good to hear
him say that.

We watched him put the flask away again, then with the same
contented look on his face said, "While I can admire your com-
mitment to Gus and the banker, I think this is not the place you
want to be. Death comes three ways here: quick, cheap, and
easily. As you might have witnessed a bit ago when those two
unfortunates were dispatched. It was a ghastly, but too common
of a sight in this place. I sometimes wonder if the Lord meant
for me to come here to reform these poor souls, or, to tell me
my time was up and show me the true gates to hell."

He stood then and went to the tent's opening and, without
turning to us, added: "This here is a death trap for anyone who
is unprepared for such violent acts, and even those who are.
The worst of the worst seek succor here to avoid capture by the
law, and in turn, two, gun-toting lads such as yourselves; for
you to go up against the likes of One-eye Texas Jack Crowfoot
and his bunch, well, my advice is to climb aboard your cayuses
and ride for all you're worth and don't look back."

"We can't," I said. "We made a promise and our word is our
bond."

Preacher remained vigilant at the tent's opening.

"Take my advice. This banker can find himself a new wife
and Gus will get buried one way or the other, and as for the
two of you, go home and remain there. You're both too young
to be put asunder in a cold dark grave, like your friends."

I corrected him by saying that the Pallor boys were not
friends, but assassins we'd hired and assassins only. That they

were the only ones we could find to take on the job and that no matter their murderous past, we still felt sorry they'd been killed.

"Ain't that right, Albert?"

Albert nodded, but not enthusiastically.

"We aimed to split Mr. Pettymoney's reward with them," Albert said.

Still looking outward, Preacher said: "Do you even know if this woman is alive, or here?"

We shook our collective heads.

"We were wondering if you might have seen her," I said, reaching for the small framed photograph Mr. Pettymoney had given me, then realized I'd lost it in our flight from the Indians.

"Mr. Pettymoney had given me a photograph of her but I lost it."

"She's pretty," Albert said.

"Would she possibly have been the one sitting on my lap?" he said.

"No, Mrs. Pettymoney had light-colored hair, not dark like the one riding your knee bone," Albert said.

"Well, boys, I only arrived here a few days ago, so I couldn't say I've seen anyone close to fitting the description, but then again, I ain't quite got around to seeing all the females here about."

I swear that with the way the lantern light fell on Preacher's face all golden like, and with his longish curls and moustache and chin spade, he looked the spitting image of a picture of the Lord I seen hanging in the rectory at the orphanage. Or, Buffalo Bill.

Sister Mary Virgin had talked about how the Lord would return again but maybe in a different body, so it made me wonder for the briefest moment if it was possible, Jesus and Preacher was the same one. But I quickly dispelled of that idea when Preacher reached into his pocket and took out the flask again for a tipple.

Such thinking led to other thinking, as it most always does with me. Sister told me I had an active mind. So I devised a plan. I would go and stand watch outside the saloon and wait for One-eye to come out, and then follow him to whichever shack he lived in, figuring if Mrs. Pettymoney was in camp, that's where I'd find her. I told Albert and Preacher of my plan.

"I've heard worse plans," Preacher said.

"I dunno," Albert said. "Sounds dangerous, especially if he was to spot you dogging him."

"It's nice and dark," I said, "How's he gonna spot me, the color I am? 'Sides, he's most likely to be drunk."

"He still might spot you," Albert said. "You don't know what kind of eyes he's got. He could have those evil eyes can see in the dark, like the devil himself."

"He's only got one eye in that big head of his, and I'm betting it is the same as everybody else's, ain't that right, Preacher?" I said, seeking confirmation.

"I wouldn't know if his eye is or ain't able to see in the dark," Preacher said. "But Albert's right, it is dangerous, because you saw what he did at the saloon, and listen to that, they're still taking potshots at those tragic boys."

It was true. Every minute or two a gun would pop off.

"It's either I go or you go, Albert."

"Let's flip for it."

So we did and I called heads and I won, or rather I lost, and said I'd go. I guess winning and losing is all how you look at it.

"I'm not back in say an hour, just don't let 'em hang me in that tree by my feet alongside the Albinos to be taking potshots at," I said. "And if I had a ma, I'd ask you to write her a letter of my demise, but I ain't, so no point."

"We won't let them hang you in that tree," Albert said and Preacher nodded in agreement. "And if you had a ma, we'd surely write to her as well."

"Promise," I said.

"I promise," Albert said.

"Preacher?"

"I promise, also, but, Ivory, you must know that once you are dead you won't know or feel a thing, so why does it matter about getting potshot at?"

"There's no guarantee I won't know, Preacher. Not even you can speak of the nature of death and what it is and what it ain't. And besides, it seems indecent to be drilled full of holes like those Pallor brothers."

"Murder *is* indecent no matter which form it takes," Preacher reminded me, though he needn't have.

"All right, see you shortly, I hope."

I felt all fluttery inside, but left out and made my way to the far edge of the wood to where I could keep an eye on the front of the saloon. It was still lively inside, judging by the commotion of yelps and shrills and curses and glass crashing. But what drew my attention most was, there were two or three drunks standing outside there by the big cottonwood blasting away at the bodies of the Pallors, of which I was glad I couldn't see the full results of on account of the gloaming, but I could hear the ropes twist that they hung from creaking every time one of them turned this way or that as the results of being struck by gunfire. I wanted to run over there and coldcock the drunken devils just to get them to stop shooting. I was so awful mad I was near to crying.

Finally, I saw a small group of men emerge from the saloon and one of them much larger than the other and I knew by his size and deep-throated voice that he was One-eye Texas Jack. They stood talking for a few seconds, then broke up and started their separate ways. I eased out of my hidey-hole and started to follow One-eye, who walked with the steadiness of a man on

the rolling deck of a ship in a storm. I did not follow long before
a raging commotion descended upon the encampment—a commotion I knew far too well and one I had hoped my ears would
never hear again.

Indians!

CHAPTER 13

Suddenly, out of the dark they charged, whooping and hollering like fiends as the thunderous hooves of their ponies became a drumbeat on the encampment. Screams! Lordy, there were screams like you never heard if you never heard raging wild Indians attacking a bunch of white fellers.

Gunfire. Lots and lots of gunfire, as if they was trying to kill the night itself and every living thing in camp.

Something snatched my hat clean off my head and nailed it to the side of a privy: A feathered arrow clean through the crown. Folks was running every which way and where there was light, I seen them coming through the windows of the saloon; it was a mass of crazed shadows so you couldn't tell friend from foe. But then again, everybody but Albert, Preacher (and Mrs. Pettymoney if she was there) was the foe!

The air was filled with gunfire—revolvers, rifles, and shotguns, so that it sounded like the fourth of July. I heard several *thunk, thunks,* which I reckoned was arrows being shot into the hanging bodies of the Albinos. Seemed like those fellows weren't going to get any relief, even in death.

I ran and made my way back to the Sibley tent where Preacher and Albert were out front kneeling and blasting away at the darkly moving shadows.

"Don't shoot!" I yelped as I came up. "It's me, Ivory."

I got down with them.

"Good thing you said something," Preacher said between

pulling the trigger and levering his Winchester rifle, "else we might have killed you instead of the Indians or worse, One-eye."

"Don't see's how it would make a difference who killed me, but I'm glad it wasn't you two."

"Aw, he wouldn't have hit you anyway, Ivory," Albert chimed in. I knew what he meant, me being dark as the very night.

"Which way did they attack from?" Preacher said.

"All over, it sounded like," I said.

"I can't believe this is the second time me and Ivory have been attacked by Indians!" Albert said; then he cocked back the hammer of his gun and pulled the trigger and it spit fire and kicked back.

"Don't take it personal," Preacher said. "Anybody who's not Indian is fair game. If it was say, Mormon country, I reckon it would be Mormons attacking us instead."

"I reckon it don't matter," I said.

We could see them running past the far end of the woods between us and the saloon and every once in a while a bloody scream rose above all the other screams to let you know somebody had gotten it pretty good and it sort of did something to your innards to hear such screams.

"All this country used to belong to them," Preacher said. "Till we stole it."

"That's probably why they're upset," Albert said, reloading his gun.

I doubt any of us even came close to hitting anything human, red or white, but it made us feel more secure just to be shooting.

"Far as I'm concerned," I said, "they can have it back. All we've run into is trouble since coming here."

There was a constant bark of guns marked by flashes of fire coming from gun barrels like big lightning bugs that was soon added to by several of the hovels set afire with flames licking the night air.

"Looks like they intend on burning the whole show down," Preacher said, "and I'm out of bullets. I never planned on coming here to fight a war. All I wanted was to have rest and meditate."

"That's all you came here for?" Albert asked.

"Well, maybe to drink a little and consort with willing women, and preach about the evils of such things. For who knows better about sin than the sinner."

A couple of arrows clattered through the trees but fell harmlessly to the ground.

"I'm nearly out of bullets too," Albert said.

"Hold your fire then," I said, "we ain't hitting nothing anyway."

So, we held our water and Preacher took out his flask and again offered it to us but we declined, much to his relief, I suspect, since he'd shaken it to his ear and there didn't sound like all that much in it.

The fight seemed all out in front of us anyway and not getting nearer and I was glad Preacher had pitched his tent where he had and was already thinking about a new title for a dime novel: *Deadly Escape*. Oh, it might need some punching up, but it was a start. I figured if we ever got back to Last Whisky, Albert and me, we'd put our heads together and write down our exploits as we remembered them. Of course, I hadn't mentioned any of this to Albert yet, because there was every chance we might still end up like the Pallors. And even if we got out alive, I knew Albert didn't care much for more than fishing and hunting and hated schoolwork like the black plague; so I wasn't sure I could get him to throw in with me as scribes.

"We best get on back away from here," Preacher said, "just so we don't get killed, accidental or otherwise."

We eased on back farther into the trees and laid down flat and listened to the attack, savage and brutal as it was and not much we could do about it, even when we heard the terrified screams of women.

I knew it was dreadful of me to picture one of those Indians carrying off some of them big gals was in the saloon. I imagined they'd have a hard time trying to grab them up and onto their mounts.

The shooting and howling continued on for maybe twenty minutes more, and fires illumed the sky but then almost as suddenly as it had started, there were a few last yips and one or two more gunshots and things went dead quiet but for some painful moans and here or there a child crying. The Indians had disappeared off into the night where they'd come from. We could tell by their fading voices and the thundering hooves of their ponies.

The three of us rose up and eased on down into the central part of the encampment where the saloon stood with flames jumping out of its roof. A most horrible sight greeted our eyes: the corpses of the Pallor brothers were burning, blackened and charred from having been set afire.

I heard somebody in the gathered crowed of armed men say: "They saw them two as demons and lighted them up."

And just as he said it, the ropes holding the Albinos broke and they crashed to the ground in smoldering heaps. Albert and me ran to a horse tank and grabbed wood buckets and doused them and repeated the process twice more till we had them poor suckers doused and it was an awful sight to gaze on. What was once men, no matter they were Albinos and different than most other men, lying there in the tarry shapes of something akin to human. It was maybe the worst thing I ever saw.

Meanwhile those in the camp not killed—and there were several lying about filled so full of arrows they looked like large dead porcupines—had gathered in front of the burning saloon as a brightly lit backdrop for One-eye Texas Jack, who was once again the center of attention and raising the biggest ruckus.

"Who is with me?" he yelled.

Nobody said anything.

"Those dirty skins took something of mine and I aim to get her back, who's coming with me?"

The word *her* made me sick. First, she'd been kidnapped by One-eye, and now raging Indians and I was thinking Mrs. Pettymoney's—Tittey's—luck was running as bad as the Albinos, almost.

One-eye turned all about staring at the gathered.

Silence, shuffling of boots, a horse snorting.

Albert, Preacher, or myself could have shot him just then; he made the perfect target and unsuspecting, and considering his audience I don't think anyone would have objected to one more casualty that night if we had.

He ran that singular eyed stare at every man in the bunch and in turn they all studied the ground, the toes of their boots, the dead lying around.

"All right, you sons of dogs!" he growled. "One hundred dollars a man to help me get back what's mine!"

The mention of money caused hands to come out of pockets and shoot into the air like they were in a classroom for cutthroats and One-eye was their teacher asking them a history question.

"We're with you, Jack." "Count me in, Jack!" "For a hunnered dollars, I'd ride into hell with you, Jack!"

"Is it cash?" somebody said.

"What in hell else would I pay you with?" he shouted.

"Just asking," the voice replied weakly.

"All right then, grab your guns and get some horses and let's go after them rotten savages and take care of business. I'll pay an extry ten dollars for every red devil's head on a stick."

Pretty quickly all was renewed chaos of men running about and horses rearing and womenfolk trying to tend to the dead and wounded, some of them holding infants on their hips.

"They got her," I said to Albert and Preacher, "Mrs. Pettymoney. They took her from One-eye, sure enough."

"Oh, boy," Preacher said. "She won't be much to take back to her husband even if we get her back alive. I don't know it's worth it, boys. Not for me. But I'll tell you what. I'm heading down to Cheyenne and if or when you get through running over these hills chasing the redskins and kidnapped women, and you ain't killed, and you need a respite, well, look me up in the Big Horn Hotel. Otherwise I wish you all the best."

Boy, we sure hated that Preacher wasn't going to go with us, but we also understood that a man has to follow his notions, just as me and Albert had in taking up Gus and the banker's cause.

Albert and me ran and got aboard our horses and fell in with the mob of other mounted men with One-eye leading out front on a big horse with a spotted rump, and off we went into the night, in the direction they thought the marauding Indians had gone. Helping One-eye was a mixed-breed tracker I heard him call Sees Good, and every once in a while the whole contingent would stop while this fellow dropped off his horse and struck a match, holding it low to the ground to pick up the tracks of unshod and shod mounts; then he'd practically leap on the back of his horse and off we'd go again.

This went on until noon the next day and finally, One-eye, at the behest of the tracker, had us halt by a bunch of boulders and rest the horses. It further gave us a chance to rest as well.

"I don't suppose you thought to bring something to eat?" Albert said. We'd chosen to sit apart from the lot of the others.

"Sure, I've got a big steak right here in my pocket, and over in this other one a bottle of milk, and inside my jacket—"

"All right, all right," he said wearily. "I ain't in no mood for jokes."

"I'm going to lay here and dream of a cherry pie," I said, "since you got me thinking about food."

"Dream about whatever you want," he said. "It's a free world."

"For some, maybe," I said.

"Humph!"

We laid upon the ground like the others and I could hear Texas Jack amid a knot of men as rough looking as himself, talking about getting his wife back.

Someone said, "Didn't know you was married, Jack, when'd this happen?"

"It ain't quite official yet, but it soon will be," Jack said.

"You mean you ain't bespoke your nuptials yet?"

"My what?"

"Vows?"

"I'll vow to knock in your teeth." One-eye said it like a curse.

"It isn't LuLu, is it?" somebody else said. "The one with the moustache?"

"No, it ain't Lulu, you damn'd twit. When'd you ever see me doing anything with her? I wouldn't touch her if she had gold coins for eyes, and besides, she don't even like men."

"I can vouch for that," another voice said.

"How would you know, Dirty Dave?" still another one said.

"Count of I tried my best to get her to go out back of the saloon with me one night and she wouldn't go even though I offered her two damn dollars."

"Well, I guess that proves it, then," another laughed. "Imagine a woman going anywhere with you, Dirty Dave, for two whole dollars!"

Laughter all around.

And they kept up like that for a time until at last weariness and a lot of last night's liquor and all night and half a day more ride took hold of them and shut their yaps and for once it was sort of peaceful.

"How are we supposed to get her away from this mob even if we catch those danged Indians?" Albert said in a low voice edged with weariness and doubt.

"I don't know, exactly," I said. "Get some rest. I'll figure something."

"You always do, Ivory. You always do." And then he was snoring like a faulty steam engine. But he was far from that, and I was too. I told myself if we ever made it back to Last Whisky, I wasn't ever leaving again, no matter what.

No, sir. If I had to, I'd send for a mail-order woman when I got old enough to want to marry. Have her come on the train like some of them old widowed codgers did.

Then, suddenly, I was in a room with red wallpaper and a beautiful brown sugar of a girl wanting to kiss me and beckoning me to come closer by crooking her finger at me and with the most alluring smile on her lips and her teeth was as white as a sunlit cloud.

Then *bang!*

I was jarred awake by the loudest boom I ever heard.

And so was the rest of the camp.

We were lying under an inch of new snow and there was crashing thunder and lightning shooting out of a fog-dense sky. And suddenly a screeching cry of "Dirty Dave's been kilt!" and we turned our attention to a dead horse with its rider still in the saddle lying on the ground. Apparently, he had been guarding the camp in case the Indians doubled back on us.

This Dirty Dave's legs were wrapped around the cayuse's gaunt belly and held fastened by the fact his spurs had been fused together from an obvious lightning strike. The man's long black hair was also afire and some of the boys were scooping up handfuls of snow to douse it.

As we got nearer, we could see a blackened ill-shapen burn hole on the side of the rider's cheek. His eyes were open as if surprised, and I thought, *No doubt he surely was.*

"Lightning hit him atop the head and came out the side of his face," a skinny fellow wearing a black hat said. "I seen something like it before one time in the Texas Panhandle. Kilt fifty cattle as well as two nighthawks."

The storm continued to dance around us as we made ourselves small in among some boulders. As soon the danger became a reality, some of us might join Dirty Dave and his horse if we didn't make ourselves small, so that is what we did, getting in among the rocks.

We could hear Texas Jack cussing somewhere in the swirl of snow and sleet and utter chaos and for a good half hour more the storm raged as if discontent with killing just one rider and his horse, but then slowly marched off to the east.

"This sure is a miserable situation," Albert said.

"Misery is starting to sound like our middle name," I added.

"Ain't it, though," said the same skinny fellow wearing a black hat who claimed he'd seen lightning kill horses, cattle, and men in Texas, as he got down alongside Albert and me. His face was cruel and his lower lip hung out oddly.

"Don't believe I know you two," he said and stuck out his paw. "Name's Jim Miller, some calls me Deacon Jim, and some calls me Killer Miller, but, aw hell, what care I of such appellations?"

"I'm Ivory," I said, "and this is Albert," and we shook his paw and little did we know of this fella's reputation till later on having read in the *Police Gazette* about his being hanged for a host of crimes in a barn in Ada, Oklahoma, still wearing the same black hat. There was even a photograph of him and two or three others dangling from a beam. It put a little ice water in you to read something like that about a fellow you know, or should I say, knew?

This Miller asked if we had a match to light the cheroot he'd put into his mouth and held clenched with yellow teeth whilst looking over toward the lightning-struck horse and rider. We told him that, no, we didn't have a match. Some of the others debated how to extract this Dirty Dave from his horse.

At first, they tried to pull the dead man's boots off but they wouldn't come off the way his feet were knotted and crooked at the ankles. They thought about trying to cut the horse in half but decided that was going to be too much work. Then this Jim Miller, who had gotten himself a light for his cheroot, went over there puffing away and opined that they should cut Dave's legs off; it was the only way, he said.

There was great debate about that: Dave's friends wishing them not to mutilate him further, saying it would be unseemly. I was impressed by the use of that word, "unseemly," especially coming from some outlaw's mouth.

"He won't feel it," Jim Miller, or Deacon Jim, or Killer Miller, said. "He's dead. The dead don't feel nothing. I know on account of I've buried a lot of them, and not a single one put up a protest." Which caused a few of the gathered to snort.

Some of them standing around observing the situation and scratching their chins and scrawny necks and crotches, as men will tend to do when faced with a conundrum (another fine word Mr. Webster put in his book), offered differing opinions and at last Mr. Miller said, "Well, if you chickenshits can't make up your minds, just leave the poor fellow to nature's wonderments and sooner or later the wolves and coyotes and weather well take care of Dirty Dave here, and his fine-looking horse. Crows love eyeballs and I reckon they'll be taken first."

Finally, Miller drifted off again. Somebody had built a fire and put on a pot of coffee to boil because one of them had thought in advance that we might be gone for more than half a day.

Albert and me came in as close as we dared but managed to get a cup of coffee as we tried our best to learn what was going to happen next. One-eye had sent the tracker off to look for the raiding Indians' trail, for, as he said, "I don't aim to wander around in this snow blindly searching for damn no-good red-skins who would steal from me, but I do aim to find them and kill them just as soon as that scout can locate their trail. And I aim to kill them with all deliberation when I do find them, for they took from me what is mine."

Somebody piped up and said, "Hell, Jack, if it's just a woman, why, you can just get you another any time."

"Not like this one," he growled. "She's special."

"What's so special about her, Jack? Why all the ones I seen have the same parts, just different names and hair color is all."

Some started to laugh, then they shut up just as quickly when One-eye did not so much as crack a smile.

And so we waited until near nightfall for the tracker to return.

Then Killer Miller turned and walked back over to where me and Albert now squatted by the rock sharing the single cup of coffee.

Even though I didn't smoke, nor did Albert, the smell of that cigar on such clear brittle air gave me the hankering to try it someday soon. I thought it also made a fellow look manly—even this Jim Miller—and maybe if I was to take up the habit, the gals might see me as more manly too.

"Them boys is a bunch of bona fide Nancies," Jim Miller said, grinning around the cheroot. I don't think I ever seen a smile more bereft of compassion.

"What's your assessment of that situation yonder?" he asked.

"Like you said," I replied. "Best to leave it to nature. Sure wouldn't care to see a man's legs cut off just in order to bury him."

"Aw, hell, they wouldn't bury him no way. Got no shovels. They're just yammering because they're as dumb as hammers and don't know how to do nothing else but yammer."

He leaned and spat after taking the cheroot from his mouth and eyed me careful.

"What's a black child like you and your blond-haired friend here doing with this pack of mongrels? You both look innocent as schoolgirls."

I straightened so he could get a good eyeful of the handle of my revolver sticking out of my holster, and Albert followed my lead, like we most always did when we were a little afraid and didn't want to seem like we were.

"We rode into Robbers Roost looking for a fellow we was chasing. Me and Albert here is bounty hunters," I lied, recalling what Sister Mary Virgin told me by saying: "Ivory, every person is given one particular gift by the Lord they will carry with them forever." She was right. Mine was the gift of artful lying.

"Oh, who'd that be?" Killer Miller, or Deacon Jim if you prefer, said.

I saw the way Albert was looking at me, and of course I could not let him down. So I said, "He goes by the name Red Dog, but that's just one of his aliases," I said. "He's a murderous scoundrel that raised holy havoc throughout the Nations. Robbed banks, trains, stagecoaches, slapped around children, and even violated little old women."

"At least three we know of," Albert chimed in and I was proud that I was not only helping to improve his vocabulary, but teaching him when to lie.

"Albert and me heard he might come to the Roost to seek refuge," I continued. "Why, with such a huge reward on his head, the man that gets him is going to be powerful rich."

Mr. Miller stood watching me close for a full minute, then hawked and spit again before reinserting that nasty looking chewed cheroot back in his mouth.

"Well, what does he look like?" Killer Jim said.

I swallowed hard.

"You know," I said. "To be truthful, he looks a lot like that big fellow yonder, the one with the patch over his eye and cussing all the time."

Killer Jim looked over at One-eye Texas Jack.

"His name ain't Red Dog," he said.

"What is it, then?" Albert asked.

"Why, that there is One-eye Texas Jack Crowfoot," Killer Jim said, but I could tell by the way he was watching One-eye he had begun to suspect that just maybe, One-eye might not be who he said he was.

"Well, like I said," I replied. "Red Dog's been known to use many aliases. Have you known Mister Crowfoot a long time?"

"A week, maybe, since I come into camp."

"So, it is entirely possible that he's got other names," Albert said, stirring Mr. Killer Miller's beans like only he can do once he gets into the flow of things.

"How much you say is that reward money?"

"Upwards of ten thousand dollars cash money, *dead* or alive. Fact is, I think the law would just as soon he be brought in belly down to save the expense of several trials for all his crimes."

"Heck, they get him back they'll just hang him, anyway," Albert said. "So, it won't matter much how he's brought in."

Boy, we could see the wheels turning in Killer's brainpan as clearly as if it had been written on his forehead in India ink.

"Well that is right interesting," Killer said. "But listen here, that's a mean, merciless man you boys are speaking of and he'd just as soon kill you and eat you for dinner as to look at you. I was there in the saloon when he drilled them Albinos, and you surely seen how he had them strung up afterwards so the boys could take potshots."

I pretended to shiver and Albert did his best impression of shaking in his boots.

"Don't matter, Mister Miller," I said. "We need that money to save our farm."

"Yeah, well, sonny, out here on the frontier, it's every man for himself." Then Killer stood and walked away while Albert and me watched.

Just about then Sees Good, the scout, came riding into camp and slid off the back of his horse and went to the fire around which most the others had hunkered down. He knelt down next to One-eye and spoke into his ear.

Me and Albert were sitting too far away to hear what it was he whispered in Jack's ear but the big fool looked up with his mouth agape and somebody else said, "What is it, Jack?"

"Scout here says she got away."

"What?"

"How could that even be?"

"Scout here says them dirty redskins got to fighting over her as to whose wife she was to be, and things got plenty heated and knives and guns were pulled and they commenced to cutting and shooting one another, and while they were slaughtering each other she snuck off and made the wagon road."

He paused and looked at the tracker again.

"Tell 'em what you done told me," One-eye said to the tracker.

"I tracked her to the stage road by a bloody trail in the snow and found one of them alive, but was half dead until I killed him and made him all dead. But, before I killed him, he said he'd followed her even though he was shot and bleeding, figuring since he was the only one left of their bunch that the white woman rightfully belonged to him."

The scout got himself a cup of coffee and held it in both hands for a moment, then sipped some as he continued his tale.

He said the stage came along just as he about caught up with her and she waved it down. Still he tried to get hold of her but the driver fired a gun at him and the buckshot broke both his legs. So, he just laid down in the snow and waited and sang his death song.

"How you know the skin wasn't lying to you?" One-eye said to the scout.

The scout took his time, drinking more of the coffee, for it was powerfully cold by then.

"I had my knife to his throat and said I'd cut his apple out. He said what would be the point to lie now that his brothers were all dead and he was almost. The last thing he said before I cut out his apple was: 'Men are such damn fools over women.' "

"That's it, then?" somebody said. "We can go back to Robbers Roost and let all this go. That dead Injin was right—we *are* such damn fools."

"There's plenty more to be done in, I reckon," said another.

They started to gather up their things and saddle their mounts. They were heading back to the Roost and I can't tell you what a relief it was to hear Mrs. Pettymoney had got away.

One-eye stood and cussed them for being cowards.

"Nancies!" he screamed, which I am sure didn't do much for his cause with that bunch.

Somebody piped up and said, "Hell, Jack, she's just a woman, why, you can get you another any time, just find you a wedding and snatch her up."

Laughter. Guffaws. Hoots

"No! I want this one!" Texas Jack growled.

"Ah hell, Jack, she's just a woman. Let it go and git you another!" One-eye glared at the man who'd spoken up and I thought he might just shoot him, though it would be no great loss to mankind if he had, I imagined, for they were all outlaws, brigands, and yellow dog curs, and one less might improve humankind.

"She's a virgin, is what's so special," One-eye shouted. "She's still a virgin and will be until we get married."

Our ears perked up, Albert's and mine and I whispered: "He's not violated her."

"Dang. Talk about miracles," Albert said. "See, Ivory, I knew the good Lord was watching over her."

"And us, too, maybe a little," I said.

Some of them started to snigger and some started to laugh, then they shut up just as quickly when One-eye jerked his guns and started trying to kill the air with them. The sky slaying only hastened the boys stepping feet into stirrups and riding off.

"Come back here you dirty—"

Bang!

I suppose Albert and me could have shouted a warning to One-eye that there was a fellow by the name of Jim Miller, or Killer Jim Miller, sneaking up on him with a cocked revolver in hand and aimed at the back of One-eye's large skull, but for once the circumstances had silenced our tongues, and instead we watched with interest the demise of One-eye Texas Jack Crowfoot as the top of his head shattered like an egg thrown against a brick wall.

He was in mid-cuss, which somehow seemed proper.

"Karma," I said.

"What?" Albert said. "Caramel? What's that have to do with anything?"

"I'll explain it later," I said.

We watched Killer Miller load One-eye's bulk onto the back of his horse; then he mounted his own after looping a lead rope to the Appaloosa and wave to us.

"You snooze, you lose, boys!" he called. "Next time you're

after a fellow, keep it to yourselves is my advice. You're looking at a newly rich man. Hidey Ho!"

We watched him ride off with the body of a man Albert and me both held in low regard and felt neither sadness nor joy.

Then mounting our own horses, I was thinking about how fate had indeed intervened and whether it was the Lord's doing or not and decided that it really didn't matter as long as the results were the same.

For several years at the orphanage, the sisters had tried to get me to see and understand what it is the Lord wants of all of us and mostly it didn't stick too much with me, preferring as I did to put my trust in Messer's DeWitt and Beadle and their dime novels for my happy outlook, and Mister Webster for my ongoing education and giving me the idea of becoming a writer.

CHAPTER 14

We followed the southern stagecoach road to Cheyenne talking about our loss of the reward money, but feeling cheerful that Mrs. Pettymoney would eventually get home to her husband, safe and intact, so to speak. I was sure that Mr. Pettymoney held up his end of the bargain and had paid for Gus a good funeral and right that instant, Gus was resting in his eternal home, free from all trouble and strife as well under six feet of sod with a proper resting place, with no more trials and tribulations to face, including growing old like some of them folks in the homes.

"I guess we screwed the pooch as for the reward money, huh?" Albert said as the shimmering mountains of Cheyenne hove into view.

"We didn't screw anything," I reminded him. "Such events can neither be foretold nor prevented. As you yourself once said, it is all writ in the book of life long before now."

"I suppose," Albert said. "For who am I to argue against my own argument."

"You wouldn't be the first, nor the last," I said. 'Sides, look at it this way: We ain't dead and we got all our body parts still. Why, just think of those Pallor boys. I reckon they never could have imagined such an end and you and me is still breathing good clean air."

"You ever wonder about dying?"

"Sometimes."

"If you had to choose between knowing when you would die, or how you would die, which would you choose?"

"Why all this wondering about death?" I said.

He shrugged and said, "I don't know, but it strikes me that no matter what sort of life a body lives, we all end up in the same way, don't we, Ivory?"

"True enough. Someday we'll be dead, but it ain't the dying, I reckon that counts so much as what happens between now and the dying that matters."

"I suppose," he said, unenthusiastically, I thought, for a feller who had escaped almost certain death at least twice now.

"What's got you so morose?" I said.

He cut me a mean look.

"Means gloomy. I'd think you'd be happy as a pig running out the back of a butcher shop."

"I was just thinking about Geneva Pearlfeather," he said. "You know."

"Sure, but heck, you're soon going home to your sweetheart," I said.

"You're right, I almost forgot."

We crossed a river at the shallows with the sun sparkling in it like broken shards of glass and all in all it was wonderful looking country and I started wondering once I got back to Last Whisky if I'd stay there much longer than to eat some good meals at Albert's ma's place and get some good sleep. For now that I had seen more of the country, I wondered what the rest looked like. I was growing and my thinking was changing as it will with any boy, I reckon. Albert was changing too, getting tall like his father had been. His voice was getting deeper too, like a man's, and so was mine. In a way it troubled me that we were both growing up so and it might come a day when we went our own ways and I'd lose the best friend I ever had.

But this day, of all other days, Albert Sand was still the best friend I ever had and I reckon a body can't ask much more than that from life.

We'd looked up Preacher at the Big Horn Hotel like we said we would and he took us down to the fancy dining room and we all ordered steaks and ate like we were to be executed by a firing squad soon as we finished.

Between bites and sips of wine, which I liked a lot, we told Preacher the entire story about this Killer Miller busting a cap in One-eye Texas Jack Crowfoot's brain after we convinced Miller that Jack had a huge reward on him.

Preacher laughed until he near choked.

"That's the best story I've heard this year," he said.

He cut off another bite of his meat and chewed it with the greatest look of contentment on his face.

"Now, I have a story to tell you boys," he said washing down his food with more wine.

"It was all over town when the stage arrived with Mrs. Pettymoney: " 'The woman who escaped savage Indians,' is how the paper had it. I looked her up and told her who I was, that I was a good friend of yours and how you two had been trying to rescue her and so on and so forth."

Albert and me stopped chewing.

"Well, anyway, she wired her husband and then I helped her purchase new clothing, and a room at the hotel and a ticket home. She left just this morning as a matter of fact."

"That's the best dang news yet, ain't it, Ivory," Albert said.

I allowed as how it was.

Then Preacher took an envelope from his coat pocket and put it on the table.

"Once we wired her husband, he wired a deposit of the full five-hundred to the bank. She got it and asked me to give it to the two of you—minus my ten percent of course."

The envelope was full of money.

"No, that's the best danged news yet!" I said.

On the train ride home to Last Whisky, Albert and me were reading the latest dime novels, me: *DEVIL DANCE OF THE APACHES,* and Albert was reading: *BUFFALO BILL'S DEATH DROP, or THE GHOST SCOUT OF COLORADO.*

We'd purchased some taffy off a candy butcher and struggled to keep it from sticking to our teeth as we read.

We'd just gone over a bridge when Albert looked up with puzzled eyes.

"Say, Ivory, you remember you were going to explain to me that word *Karma,* I think it was?"

"Yes."

"Well, what is it?"

"Think of it this way, Albert: One-eye Texas Jack did all those horrible things to others, such as shooting out Gus's brains, and in the end, a horrible thing was done to him."

'Oh, you mean like what goes around comes around?"

"Exactly."

Albert looked pleased with his powers of reasoning, grinned like a gopher eating new grass, and went back to reading his novel.

I glanced out the window as we passed through the beauty of the West, my West, as the train's shadow chased alongside of us.

Going home, I thought.

Going home, at least for now. Me and my best friend, Albert Sand.

ABOUT THE AUTHOR

Bill Brooks lives and works in Florida and, in spite of having survived two hurricanes—Hermie and Irma—has written more than forty novels of historical fiction. When asked why he became a writer, his answer is simple: "I'm too lazy to work and too dumb to steal."

The employees of Five Star Publishing hope you have enjoyed this book.

Our Five Star novels explore little-known chapters from America's history, stories told from unique perspectives that will entertain a broad range of readers.

Other Five Star books are available at your local library, bookstore, all major book distributors, and directly from Five Star/Gale.

Connect with Five Star Publishing

Visit us on Facebook:
https://www.facebook.com/FiveStarCengage

Email:
FiveStar@cengage.com

For information about titles and placing orders:
(800) 223-1244
gale.orders@cengage.com

To share your comments, write to us:
Five Star Publishing
Attn: Publisher
10 Water St., Suite 310
Waterville, ME 04901